After the Darkness

After the Darkness

Michael Smith

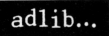 Scholastic Publications Limited

For Sabrina,
who never lost hope.

Scholastic Children's Books,
Commonwealth House, 1–19 New Oxford Street,
London WC1A 1NU, UK
a division of Scholastic Ltd
London ~ New York ~ Toronto ~ Sydney ~ Auckland

First published in the UK by Scholastic Ltd, 1996

Copyright © Michael Smith, 1996

ISBN 0 590 54260 5

Typeset by DP Photosetting, Aylesbury, Bucks.
Printed in England by Progressive Printing (UK) Limited,
Leigh-on-Sea, Essex.

10 9 8 7 6 5 4 3 2

The right of Michael Smith to be identified as the author of this
work has been asserted by him in accordance with
the Copyright, Designs and Patents Act, 1988.

1.

There was chaos in the apartment. In the middle of her bedroom a woman knelt on a rug beside a half-filled suitcase as she sorted feverishly through the disorderly piles of possessions which surrounded her.

In an adjoining room her husband was engaged in a similar task. Papers lay strewn everywhere, official-looking documents, bank statements and cheque books, birth certificates and a marriage certificate, bundles of letters and cards. Almost fourteen years of family life, stored neatly away for so long, but now, today, as the man heard the familiar shouts of soldiers in the street below, it had to be sorted into two piles. One pile to be kept and the other destroyed.

Two children ran about pretending to tidy their rooms, but they knew there was no reason to leave them tidy. They were leaving Paris and their father had said they might never come back. The children wanted to come back if they could, of course, they were Parisians and the apartment had been their home for as long as either of them could remember, but their father had wanted to prepare them for the worst. So the children ran about, not in joy nor any sort of happy mood, more in panic at the realization that their lives in the apartment were coming to an end. They were leaving home.

In all the rooms pictures had been taken from the walls, ornaments had been swept aside and half-empty drawers pulled to the floors, their contents scattered about as if a violent windstorm had struck the building or the apartment had been ransacked by burglars.

"What do we do with passports?" the man called to his wife. "And birth certificates? Should we hide them in case we ever need them again, or do we destroy them so there's no evidence of who we were? I don't know. I just don't know what to do, or what to expect."

He wore a dark suit and a tie and his black shoes were highly polished. His name was Cohn, M. Leon Cohn. Before the war he had been a lawyer, a successful lawyer too, but the arrival of the Germans had changed all that. He had not worked for almost two years now and the strain of pretending to carry on a normal life in Paris had begun to show. His handsome face had grown drawn and lined and his head bore more grey hairs than might have been expected for a man of only thirty-eight.

But he had a dignified look about him still, despite the frantic air in the house, and in spite of his doubts about what to throw away and what to keep he worked methodically, calling to his wife from time to time, more to reassure her he was still there than because there was anything they needed to discuss.

They had begun to make their plans almost two years ago, on the last day of September 1940 in fact, three days after the Germans had taken control of Paris and northern France. M. Cohn had known straight away they would have to go, of the problems they would face if they stayed. They were Jews and life was bound to become difficult for Jews in France once the Nazis got control.

"We need to plan this very carefully," he had told his wife, "and we must plan it now, while we can still buy petrol and food. We should sell the apartment, the furniture, the pictures, anything valuable we have. All we will need is the car and enough petrol to get us to Spain, if Spain will take us, that is."

"How can you be so sure this war will last that long?" Madeleine Cohn had asked her husband. "It might be all over in a few months."

"It might, yes," M. Cohn had replied, "but the Germans might win it and if they do, or even if they lose, it will be bad for us. I think we will be in great danger. I don't know when we will need to go, but we must be ready. We will stay as long as we can and we will prepare ourselves, but one day we will have to go. I am sure of that."

That day M. Cohn had started planning their escape. He bought as much petrol as he could and stored it in cans in a wardrobe in their daughter's bedroom. He knew the dangers of this, but what else could he do? They had no garden shed, not even a garden, and the balconies of their apartment had open iron railings and anyone could see up through them without difficulty. The only secure place was in a bedroom.

His wife hoarded tins of food and packets of powdered milk. They put aside warm clothes and blankets, and soap and toothpaste for the journey they knew they would have to make.

Leon Cohn was a practical man. He was always able to see what lay ahead and all his life he had been ready. Madeleine, his wife, was less sure of the future. Often she did not want to know what might be in store for them. She enjoyed being surprised by events, confident of her ability to react quickly to whatever might happen. But in this matter of the war she let her husband have his way. There were the children to think of, and her old mother. She knew she could not leave their futures to chance. She was sad, though. She loved Paris. She would have preferred never to leave. Paris was her home.

During that summer of 1940, before the Armistice was signed, Mme. Cohn's brothers had fled with their families to the south-west, to Bordeaux, pretending they were going on a long holiday, and at the end of summer, after the Armistice had been signed, they had tried to return to Paris only to be turned back by the Germans. Only non-Jews could come back to the German-occupied sector, they had been told. They had run away from Paris. They were Jews and they had run away. Now they must stay away.

They were Jews, the Nazis kept saying. How could they possibly be considered loyal to the new France? So they had turned back, to the south this time, to Avignon, where M. Cohn, their brother-in-law, had family, but they had gone with no money, nowhere to live, with nothing at all. Mme. Cohn had had no word from them for many months.

Instead of leaving Paris in the summer of 1940, M. Cohn had had the car serviced. It was a Citroën, almost new, and they had hardly used it at all during the next two years. It was in good condition and they had hoarded enough petrol to get them to Spain. They had a little money left too, although there was no certainty it would be any use for much longer, and they had planned carefully what they would take in the car. The children could fit into the back seat with a bundle of clothes on each of their laps. The two larger trunks would fit into the boot of the car with the extra petrol, and Mme. Cohn could have a case at her feet with a few valuables in it.

They had decided not to load more things on to the roof. It would only attract attention to them, and then they would probably lose what was inside the car as well as what was on the roof. All the furniture they had not been able to sell was being left behind and only the smallest pictures were being taken. Leon Cohn had decided not to sell any of their other things. During the two years since the Germans had invaded France prices had fallen to ridiculous levels and, anyway, to be seen selling things would only have drawn attention to them. Questions would be asked about why they were selling. Were they planning to leave Paris, the Nazis would probably ask, and where might they be going? Did they have permission to do this or that, or go here or there, and why did they want to leave anyway? Life wasn't too bad in Paris was it, in the summer of 1942? As long as you had paid your fines for being Jewish that was. And France was peaceful now, wasn't it? Not like the rest of the world. Why would any true patriot want to go away?

M. Cohn knew all the questions by heart. He had paid his fines although it meant they had very little money left, but he knew there would be more fines, month after month, year after year, until he was ruined. And collection of the fines had been enforced everywhere, even in the south, in Vichy France, by the government of Marshall Pétain, the old warrior alongside whom M. Cohn's father had fought against Germany only twenty-five years before. Pétain had been a hero in those days but now he seemed to be a friend of the Germans. Nothing made sense any more. Leon Cohn was at his wits' end to understand it.

He tore a bundle of papers to shreds and tossed them away

absentmindedly. He took up an old photograph of his two children and stared at it for a while before slipping it into his pocket. It had always been one of his favourites, taken by himself a few years earlier, as they sat side by side on a single chair. How young they seemed then, he thought, and how solemn, almost as if, even then, they feared for their future together.

At the end of June 1942 came the last straw. A letter from the authorities. The Cohn's apartment was to be taken over, the letter said, to be used for official purposes. There was nothing else, no explanation. They had to be out by the fourteenth of July, Bastille Day, France's day of Liberty. Leon Cohn smiled wryly when he read that. If he had been a weaker man he might have lost hope, or even have wept, but he was strong enough to know when not to fight, when he could not hope to win, so he sighed deeply, and he and his wife finalized their plans to leave Paris.

They waited until it was almost dark before they started to load the car and they took only one case at a time down to the basement. They would stay one more night in the apartment and set off early the following morning. They would sleep in the car during their journey in order that they would not have to give their names to any hoteliers and they would stay away from restaurants. They had almost a week's supply of food, chocolate too, saved from the early days of the war, before it became impossible to find in the shops. The children had not had chocolate for almost a year now. They talked about it as if it was going to be the most exciting part of their journey. Two kilograms of chocolate, to be eaten on the way to Spain. It was all rather an adventure, really.

The two children slept quite well that night, better than their parents, but not because they were unworried. When they first went to bed they fell into an exhausted half sleep, thinking of the things they feared they would never see again, of all the things that had made the apartment their home. Pictures of the toys and possessions they were leaving behind them drifted through their minds. The colours of their rooms seemed to press down on them, somehow more intense because they knew it might be the last time they would see them. The light of the summer evening seeping through the curtains had a strange eerie glow and familiar objects in the rooms like tables or lamps took on sinister shapes, as if they were trying to disguise themselves from their owners as a punishment for deserting them.

Later in the night the children slept more deeply and in the morning they did not recall their dreams.

2.

Leon Cohn decided to make for Avignon not because he knew much about that lovely southern city, but because it was the last place in which his relations had been heard of, and there was a rumour one of them had managed to get his wife and children away safely to Spain. In any case the roads to the south-west were bound to be crowded with other refugees from Paris, too many people trying to get away in the same direction, M. Cohn said. They would be better to go as far south as possible, to the Mediterranean perhaps, before turning west and making for the Spanish border. Besides, his cousins lived near Avignon, and the Cohn family had gone there for holidays, two or three times before the war. They might have changed their address of course, but Mme. Cohn was sure there would be no difficulty in finding them, and surely they would be able to help?

So they set off for Avignon on the fourteenth of July, 1942. They would not try to do the journey too quickly, M. Cohn told them, three or four days of easy driving and no travelling at night either. They would sleep and eat at the usual times, there need be no panic, no need to hurry or attract attention to themselves, but they would need to be careful. They would tell any police who stopped them they were going south for a holiday, to get away from their apartment for a while.

It was almost seven in the morning when they began. They had hoped to leave Paris earlier but just after dawn there had been a lot of noise in the streets. Soldiers and police were everywhere, shouting and banging on doors, and military vehicles were stopped at regular intervals along the pavements, their guns menacing the early morning passers-by. "There's too much going on," M. Cohn kept saying, as he looked from their window. "It's too soon. We must wait. We must be patient. They'll be gone in a while, then we can start. Anyway," he added, to bolster his argument, "it's not as if we have anything else to do today, is it? We're going away, like all the other Jews. We're leaving Paris, leaving France. There's plenty of time for people like us." He tried to smile at his family, but even his young daughter could see he did not believe his own words.

"Could I telephone my mother one last time?" asked Mme. Cohn. "I'm desperately worried about her, about leaving her here."

"You've said your farewells," M. Cohn said. His voice was almost stern but the expression on his face was one of sorrow. He too had tried to persuade his mother-in-law to come away with them, but she had refused.

"I'm too old," she had told him. "I won't be able to keep up with you. Leave me here. My neighbours will look after me perfectly well. And when all this is over I'll be waiting here for you when you get back." She had an absolute certainty that the war would be over in a few months and that France would be free again. She had pushed Leon Cohn's hand away from her shoulder to show him how little she needed to be comforted, but her mouth had been set firm for a long time afterwards and she had not spoken for a full minute, turning her back to him and gazing into the empty fireplace, at nothing in particular.

"What if anything should happen to you?" M. Cohn had said. "What if you become ill?"

"Mme. Soubeyron and I have been friends for more than thirty years," she had replied. "We have discussed all this. If she is ill, I will look after her, and if I am ill, she will look after me. Her husband is a good man. He will keep his job and between us we should have enough money to last until this war is over. If the very worst should happen the Soubeyrons will shelter me. I can hide in their apartment. Look." She pulled her tiny shoulders close to her neck and held her arms in to her sides to make herself look as small as possible. "I'm no bigger than a large dog. They could fit me into a cupboard if necessary," she had smiled broadly, "and if the food rationing in Paris becomes worse, why, even an empty wine case might be big enough to hold me.

"I will be all right, Leon," she had told him, "and tell Madeleine not to worry either. I'm tougher than you think. You've got your children to think of, not me. They are the ones who will really suffer if you stay in France, if you don't get away. Look after them. Get them to Spain, or Canada, or England. Get them away from these Nazis and traitors who run France now. And don't worry about me. Now goodbye." She had held out her frail old arms to him and he had placed his hands on her shoulders, wondering if he would ever see her again. "I always liked you, Leon," she had said. "Not many men could have kept my daughter happy, my dear wild Madeleine. You have been a good son-in-law to me and a good husband to her. Go now. Go away from here. Away from France. And when it's all over you can bring back my daughter and my beautiful grandchildren. We'll have fun again, you'll see. Just promise me you will bring my daughter back, my darling Madeleine, and my pretty Lucie and my handsome Jean-Pierre."

M. Cohn had not been so sure. He had wanted to believe the old woman, but he was not sure the war would be over so soon, nor that the right side was going to win.

"You've said your farewells," he repeated to his wife. "It would be better to leave it at that. Your mother gets upset by all this, even if she doesn't show it."

So they did not telephone Mme. Cohn's mother that morning. They sat quietly and waited patiently in the sparsely furnished apartment which was no longer theirs, until the noises in the street had died away and the soldiers had gone, before they crept like thieves down the three flights of stairs to the basement of the building and left their home for the last time.

3.

It was a glorious day as they drove out of Paris into the countryside. Small tufts of pure white cloud scudded across the bluest of skies, driven by a gentle breeze from the north which seemed as if it had sprung up with no other purpose but to blow them all the way to Avignon. The trees fluttered their leaves in farewell, the crops in the fields swayed in a series of easy ripples and the grasses by the roadside waved gently as if a giant invisible hand was caressing them. The road to Fontainebleau was busy, but not slow, and they were able to make good speed. They passed roadblocks from time to time, but nobody caused them any problems. They had left Paris, they were going to leave the German-occupied sector of France, they were Jews who were moving out and the Germans seemed to have little interest in them.

"Don't come back," one guard scowled as he returned their papers. He turned his rifle menacingly towards the window of the car. Mme. Cohn had been about to reply when her husband put his hand on her arm to restrain her. He drove off slowly, not wanting to appear too keen to be gone.

"How dare he say that!" exclaimed his wife. "Paris is *our* city not his. This is France, *our* country. How dare he tell us not to come back!"

"Well, he did dare, didn't he," M. Cohn replied. "He had the gun. So he did dare. There are other ways of defeating these people, my dear, without challenging them when they are bound to win. We are going to have to get used to letting them have their little victories from time to time. We are refugees now. We have nowhere to go back to and nowhere to go forward to except as these people allow."

Madeleine Cohn sat quietly fuming in her seat as the beautiful July countryside stretched away to either side of them. After a while, her husband put his hand out to her and she took it in hers, kissing it and massaging it with her fingers as if it was the only thing she was aware of, and holding it tightly, first to her breast and then her lips. After a while she spoke. "Stop the car, Leon," she said at last. "Just for a minute. There's something I must say. Something I must do. Please stop the car."

As she spoke, Madeleine Cohn hardly knew what she wanted to say to her family, but she was overwhelmed by a feeling of anticipation, clouded by fear it was true, but a feeling that somehow she and her family were on the verge of some turning point in their lives. She had no idea what it might be, no vision of what the future might hold, but something was there ahead of them and she did not want to let the moment pass unspoken.

The black Citroën came to a halt alongside a copse of tall trees. The road ahead bent sharply to the right following the line of a stream, before doubling back and crossing a small stone bridge above the brook. There was not another car in sight. Not far above them a pair of tawny sparrowhawks beat the warm air with their wings, their bright eyes searching the ground for prey, lizards perhaps, or a young, innocent rabbit, while higher up, dark against the clear sky, an eagle soared, so distant, so remote it seemed to Jean-Pierre Cohn, gazing up at it through the car window, that it would be impossible for its quarry to be aware of any danger. It could only seem, he thought, a threat to some other distant, unknown world, not to anything near them.

Mme. Cohn got out of the car and opened the rear door. "Come on, Jean-Pierre," she said, "and you, Lucie. There is something I must say to you, and you too, Leon. Come on. Everybody out." She walked a few steps away from the car and knelt down on the ruffling grass, sitting back on her heels, her arms outstretched to her family. They assembled before her, puzzled, awaiting another instruction. "Kneel down," she ordered them. "Come on, closer. I want to be able to touch you all."

She waited, composing her thoughts before she spoke again. This time there was a half smile on her pretty face, but her voice was not as sure as the children remembered it and her throat sounded as if it might have needed clearing. "We don't live in Paris any more," she said. "You know that, don't you? We have no apartment there any longer. We have left Paris, possibly for ever, and if we can we will leave France too. We will go anywhere to get away from the people who rule France now. We were something in Paris, we Cohns, not rich, not high society, but we had our place and we had almost everything we wanted." She paused to look at each of them in turn. She even managed to smile. "But it's all gone now. We have nothing left. In a couple of days everything in the apartment will have been taken by the Nazis, even the things in your bedrooms." She paused to gaze intently at her children, to make certain they understood every word she was saying to them. "All your things. Your toys, your books, your clothes. Everything will be gone.

"All we possess now is here in the car and there is a chance we will lose all of this too, quite soon perhaps. So we have got to see ourselves differently from now on. We aren't the Cohns from Paris any more. We are the Cohns who are going to live somewhere else and we have nothing except ourselves to rely on." She looked intently, almost fiercely, at the other three members of her family before continuing: "And I know we can succeed in this because we are quite remarkable people, all four of us."

She took her daughter's hands in her own and kissed them. "Lucie," she said, "you are remarkable.

"And you, Jean-Pierre, you are remarkable, too." She kissed the top of her son's head, holding his hands firmly in hers.

"My darling Leon," she said, "you have always been remarkable." She knelt forward and, drawing her husband's face to hers, she kissed him on the lips.

Then she let his hands drop and got to her feet. "No one will ever forget us," she said. She brushed her dress back into place firmly and she spoke with such certainty that even her husband of nearly fourteen years looked at her in amazement. "We are going to survive," she went on. "We are going to live for ever. One day the whole world is going to hear about us. We may be leaving France, we may have no idea where we are going, or how we will get there, but we will never be beaten by those people," she threw back her head in the direction they had come from, to the north, towards Paris, and raised her voice as if she was addressing the distant city itself, "those small people. One day they will know we have defeated them." She stopped and pushed her hair from her face.

"That's what I wanted to say to you," she said. "That's all. Now let's get back into the car. Let's drive on. There'll be somewhere nice for a picnic, don't you think, Leon, near Fontainebleau perhaps?"

4.

They stopped in a lane outside Fontainebleau that first night. Madeleine Cohn announced that she would not sleep in the car or even under a tree. "If I don't have a home any more I'll sleep beneath the stars," she said. "I'm sure our great-grandparents did, often enough too, and came to no harm either. Tonight Mme. Cohn is going to be completely homeless."

So they pulled their blankets from the car and spread them upon layers of dry grass and bracken which Jean-Pierre and his father had gathered. They drank water from a tin can which they filled from a nearby stream and Mme. Cohn delved into her bag for a bar of chocolate. The heat inside the car had melted the chocolate during the day and when she opened it, it was a shapeless mass sticking to its wrapping paper. She divided it as best she could into four equal pieces which she handed round. When they ate it was as if the chocolate was a magic potion, as if a miracle was being wrought in the small country lane near Fontainebleau. No troubles could overcome them, no fears await, no unhappy fate befall them as the rich smooth sweetness, the almost forgotten flavour, filled their hungry mouths.

Next Mme. Cohn produced a lemon and cut it in two. She wrapped one half in a paper bag and stowed it away. The other she squeezed into the water can before ordering her son to fill it again. "We'll need vitamin C too," she said. "My mother gave me her last three lemons. We'll have half a lemon every day so they should last us all the way to Spain, and we'll arrive in perfect health."

After they had eaten they walked in silence a short way along the lane. There had been two farmhouses within view when they arrived and, although there was no sign of life anywhere, the children needed no warning that they should not make their presence known. They moved through the forest of beech and oak in single file, warily, like animals of the night.

It was an evening none of them would ever forget. A still-ness lay across the land as if the earth was holding its breath. An old moon lay on a wisp of cloud like a lock of golden hair, dappling the floor of the forest with its pale light. Not a creature moved except for the four silent members of the family Cohn and not a breath of wind disturbed the trees below which they passed. They could have been alone in a world deserted by humankind. They came to a clearing where the wheels of farm machines had rutted a wide circle into the pathway and where another smaller track branched off aim-lessly into a darker part of the wood. They stood close to each other, close enough to hold hands if they had wished, but they were content not to touch. For a moment they seemed to be at peace, until a cloud darker than the rest drifted across the curl of the moon and somewhere far in the distance an owl screeched in triumph and a small animal cried out.

"No further I think," said M. Cohn. "The car is all we have now, we should stay close to it. Let's turn back."

"How empty the world feels," Lucie whispered as they made their way back to the car. "It's as if there is nothing but us in the whole of France, as if everyone has gone away." But the forest was not theirs alone. As they rounded the last turn in the pathway, a deer reared back from the black outline of the Citroën, startled into hesitation by their return, before bounding from sight across the soft-leafed floor of the woods.

"We are never alone," said M. Cohn. "Something is always waiting to take our place whenever we leave, and something else will have to make way for us wherever we arrive. Perhaps we have taken the deer's sleeping place tonight. Well, we will be gone tomorrow. It can come back then if it wants."

The forest outside Fontainebleau, so still and deserted the night before, came to life before daybreak with birdsong, the scratching of busy mice and the lowing of cattle in a field beyond the stream. Jean-Pierre collected water for breakfast and by six o'clock they had shaken the grass and ferns from their blankets and packed them away in the car.

They emerged on to the main road south as a cart pulled by a decrepit old pony drove out from a gateway on the other side of the road. The driver, a silver-haired farmer in the blue overalls of a peasant, yanked angrily at the reins and shook his fist after them as he watched the Citroën turn away. "We must have been on his land," Mme. Cohn said. "I'm glad we didn't come across him last night."

They made good time on the road. M. Cohn had planned a route which took them through a series of small towns with little to distinguish one from the other: Sens, Joigny, Auxerre, Avallon and down towards Beaune. At noon they stopped for lunch, pulling off the road into an empty field. It was a simple meal. There were two tins of fruit and the water they had brought from Fontainebleau. A merciless sun beat down on them, reddening their northern skin. The trees stood limpid as flags without a wind and butterflies danced above the heads of the crops. The grass by the roadside was already turning to straw, the green of spring driven down the stems by the parching heat of high summer, but on the damp ground below, the business of the field went on. Worms writhed from nowhere to nowhere, wood lice scurried from one scrap of shade to the next and earwigs lay in wait for ants. The heat was almost unbearable. "We're getting further south," M. Cohn remarked. "It's going to be hot in Avignon. Perhaps we should pray for rain."

But the sky was cloudless, there was no sign of a change in the weather, and when lunch was over they sped on through the smug, placid landscape.

It was late in the afternoon when they arrived at the crossing into Vichy France. The intensity of the day's heat seemed to have thickened the air, deadening the larksongs and the trilling of sparrows, numbing even the wiry brambles which lined the roadside and straggled over the remains of the wooden fence which separated the field from the car.

Inside the Citroën Madeleine Cohn had raised the spirits of her family. "Every day of this journey will be better than the last," she said as they left Avallon. "Every day we are further from Paris we are closer to wherever it is we are going. Within an hour or so we will be leaving the Germans behind us. We will be in the real France again. Perhaps we can stop at a restaurant, sleep a night in a hotel? We might even be able to speak to people instead of behaving like outcasts." She distributed more chocolate as an indication of her confidence in their future, she smiled from the car window as the fields and trees and houses of the German zone fell behind them. She smiled all the way to the border.

The limit of the German-occupied zone was marked by a rudimentary barrier across the road and a small green-painted hut bearing signs in French and German which indicated its purpose. Five German guards manned the border post, four of them elderly men, uncomfortable in their drab, grey uniforms. M. Cohn thought they looked like postmen or bus conductors taking part in a play, who had somehow been put into the wrong costumes.

The fifth was younger, a tall, proud Lieutenant who retired into the hut to inspect M. Cohn's papers while his men stood waiting by the car. Jean-Pierre and Lucie sat self-consciously upright as instructed by their father. "Don't try to be invisible," he had told them. "Sit up in your seats. We are doing nothing wrong, we are guilty of nothing. If you look frightened they will only become more difficult. We should look confident but not arrogant."

In a couple of minutes the Lieutenant emerged slowly, the documents of the Cohn family dangling easily from his hand as if they were of little importance. His movements were languid as he walked to the open window of the car. He wore dark-lensed glasses from behind which he appeared to stare at them for a long time. At last he spoke. "Please turn off your engine," he said. For a big man his voice was light, almost melodic. He waited, still staring, until the noise of the car's motor had died away. "Where are you going?" he continued.

"To Avignon," replied M. Cohn. "We have relations there."

There was another silence as the Lieutenant considered his

reply. He was standing upright beside the car, not bothering to stoop to the window. "And why did you leave Paris?" he asked.

"I'm sorry." M. Cohn spoke nervously. "I can't hear you."

The Lieutenant asked the question again, still with his mouth some way from the car window, but louder this time.

"It is July," M. Cohn said. "We always go away in July and August. Paris is so hot. It is very uncomfortable there. We have only a small apartment with no garden. In Avignon my family has a large garden, there is plenty of space..."

The young German lowered his face to peer into the car. "You're a Jew, aren't you?" he said. "You're a Jew and you're running away."

"I'm not running," M. Cohn told him, trying his best to maintain an even voice and angered that he should be treated so badly in front of his children. "We always go to Avignon in the summer. We are going to the house of my cousin, he is a businessman. He lives outside Avignon, a very respectable man, everybody knows him, and his wife too. She is from Carpentras." His voice trailed off as if he could not think of anything else to say about his connections in the south of France. He held tight to his wife's hand the Lieutenant noticed, as if to give himself confidence, or perhaps to keep her quiet.

But Madeleine Cohn was not used to remaining silent while her husband was being insulted. "You are absolutely correct, Lieutenant," she interrupted, leaning forward in her seat. "We are Jews, all four of us, and we are going to Avignon. There is a shortage of food in Paris, so really we are helping the German war effort, aren't we, by going to the Free

Zone? There will be more for you to eat with us gone." She let her eyes rest for just longer then necessary on the well-filled tunic of the young soldier before continuing. "Please let us through. We still have a long way to go and it's very hot in here."

The Lieutenant leant forward to rest the heels of his hands on the rim of the open window. He pushed his head through into the car, at the same time crushing the papers of the Cohn family in his clenched fist. "There is no shortage of food in Paris, Madame," he said. "In fact there is plenty of food all over France." He paused and drew his teeth back from his lips as if he was about to smile. "So if you aren't getting as much food as you are used to it is probably because you used to get too much, like all you greedy lot."

Madeleine Cohn drew a long, deep breath through her nose. Her husband felt her hand tense in his grip. He knew she would not be able to keep silent. "Did you know a lot of Jews, Lieutenant?" she asked, almost innocently. "Before the war, I mean. A lot of Jews who ate too much?"

The soldier let the bundle of papers fall from his hand on to M. Cohn's lap and reached behind himself slowly. He pulled a long-barrelled pistol from the holster on his hip and raised it, pointing it at Mme. Cohn's head and leaning as far as possible into the car until the tip of the gun was touching her skin. "You are quite right, Madame," he said softly. "It is hot in this car, isn't it, and you," he pushed the tip of the barrel hard against her temple, suddenly shouting so that his voice resounded throughout the car like a thunderblast, "YOU TALK TOO MUCH. For a Jewess, YOU TALK TOO MUCH." He lowered his voice again and continued. "But in front of your children, I won't harm you. We Germans don't do that sort of thing."

Jean-Pierre noticed a few beads of sweat seeping from the Lieutenant's forehead as he pulled himself awkwardly from the car, keeping his gun trained on Mme. Cohn's head all the time until he was able to stand upright. "Yes, you're quite right," he said, stretching his neck and shoulders with relief in the cooler air outside. "It is very uncomfortable in there. Now, how can I help you?" He looked thoughtfully at the ground for a few seconds before tossing the pistol high in the air and catching the barrel in his hand like a circus cowboy. Then, bending slightly in order to see the faces of the Cohn family again, he smiled and with a quick movement of his forearm brought the handle of the pistol down on the wind-screen of the Citroën, smashing a jagged hole in the glass in front of M. Cohn's face, leaving the rest of the pane shattered and loose in its frame. When the noise of the blow had sub-sided he bent down to look at them through the hole he had made. "There," he said. "You can't say we Germans don't do anything for you Jews, can you? You'll be much more com-fortable like that. Plenty of fresh air for the Cohn family running from Paris, eh?"

He stood back, motioning them with the butt of the pistol to move on. Leon Cohn began to pick fragments of broken glass from his clothes and his wife tried to pluck the sharpest pieces from where they lay strewn about on her lap and the dashboard and the seats of the car. But the Lieutenant was not prepared to give them time for that. He raised the gun, holding it threateningly above the windscreen again and indicating with a slight movement of his chin the direction they should take. M. Cohn fumbled for the crank-handle in its rack at the side of his seat. It seemed to be stuck, he was unable to lift it. He looked up at the soldier standing above him, his arm still raised, the pistol ready to come down on the car once more. He pulled again, harder, until at last the crank came free.

He opened his door slowly, his eyes all the time on the gun. The German stood as still as a statue, leaving only a narrow opening for Leon Cohn to slide from his seat, so that he was forced to walk round the soldier to get to the front of the car. Cohn inserted the crank in its slot and pulled it up sharply. It took several turns but at last the engine fired. He squeezed back past the guard into his seat and laid his white shaking hands on the steering wheel. But he did not drive off. The Lieutenant had thought of something else. He brought his head down level with the side window, a grimace on his face. He looked steadily at each member of the Cohn family in turn, so closely he might have been memorizing their features. Then his grimace turned to a smile once more. *"Don't come back!"* he hissed. *"You're finished here!"*

Except for the rush of wind through the open windscreen and the occasional crack as another piece of glass fell from it, enlarging the jagged-edged hole even more, there was not a sound in the car. Lucie sat hunched over, her head buried in her lap, as Jean-Pierre stroked the back of her neck with his hand. Madeleine Cohn held her face away from her husband, staring fixedly from her window. M. Cohn drove south, shaking his head from time to time as if unable to comprehend what had happened to them and, when eventually he spoke, it was with a voice so low and strange it seemed hardly his own. Fear and amazement combined to make him sound old and confused. "What kind of people are they?" he asked at last. "How can they hate us so much? People they don't even know." He shook his head again. "Thank God we are out of their control at last. At least the Vichy police won't be like that."

"Yes," said his wife. "We must tell ourselves that, mustn't we? Things will be better in Vichy France." She reached behind her, stretching out a hand to her daughter, taking her trembling fingers in her own and rubbing them gently. "They hate us because they fear us. They have been taught to fear us and therefore they hate us."

"Is it because we are remarkable, Maman?" Lucie asked. "Is that why they fear us?"

"No, my darling. That's not the reason." Madeleine Cohn almost smiled and wiped a handkerchief across her eyes with her free hand. "They don't know we are remarkable. Only we know that. It's our secret." She laid her hand on her husband's shoulder and looked at him until he returned her gaze. "But it's true nonetheless, isn't it, Leon? We are still remarkable, aren't we?"

M. Cohn nodded his head a few times as if to assure himself that he believed her. "We will stop soon," he said. "I don't want to go anywhere near Lyon today, or see another uniform, whoever is inside it."

"Don't be afraid, my darling." His wife pressed her fingers into the hard flesh of his shoulder. "They are only humans, like us."

"I'm not so afraid of the people," he said. "It's the hatred which frightens me. I don't understand it. I've never seen it before, so it frightens me."

"Yes," Madeleine smiled at him. "That's why I love you, Leon. Because hatred frightens you. You are an incredible man, my darling. Remarkable, in fact." She turned her eyes from him and looked eagerly from her window. "Come on now," she said. "We're across the border, we're in Free France. Let's see who can find somewhere quiet to spend the night, not a hotel I think. Somewhere with no soldiers and no police. Somewhere with no uniforms at all. We're in Free France at last. Everything is going to be much better from now on."

5.

It was mid-morning the next day when they entered Lyon. Twice they were stopped, the second time for almost an hour, as they were driving along the embankment of the Rhône beside an immensely long building of forbidding grey stone. The city was busy. Military vehicles and a few private cars rattled through the streets and pedestrians strolled at ease on the pavements. A steam train clattered by somewhere in the distance and barges plied the broad river, flat and smooth as satin as it drifted south towards the sun. Fruit stalls stood about beneath the shady trees, newspaper vendors were open for business and an elderly man stood by a rectangular wheelbarrow, brushing aimlessly at a pile of leaves and twigs as he stared at the black Citroën from Paris with its broken windscreen.

They waited nervously under a leafy plane tree as two officers of the Vichy police sat in a small kiosk studying their papers. Every few minutes one of the men would come to the doorway and look out at the car, no longer shiny, drab now, with the July dust of France clinging to its wheels and mud-guards.

After a while the younger of the two approached them, leaning in through of the car to talk to them. "You're Jews, aren't you?" he asked. His tone was not unfriendly.

"Yes," Leon Cohn replied.

"It's going to be all right. He's very slow, that's all." The policeman indicated the kiosk where his colleague sat at a tiny desk studying their papers. "You got out just in time, you know. It's very bad now for the Jews who are still in Paris."

"We left only two days ago." Mme. Cohn leant across to see the young officer's face. "Things weren't good then, but you're talking about something else, aren't you? What has happened? My mother is still there."

"I'm sorry to be the one to tell you, Madame," said the policeman. He leant forward, his hands resting on the roof of the car and his head bowed to the open window. "Not all of us agree with what is going on, you know, but I'm afraid the same thing might happen here soon. It's very bad in Paris, though. Thousands of Jews, just this morning. It was the French police too, not the Nazis, although I suppose it was the Nazis who put them up to it. I hope your mother was not taken, Madame."

"What has happened?" Madeleine Cohn almost shouted. "What do you mean 'It's very bad in Paris'? What's been going on?"

"I'm so sorry, Madame." He gave an apologetic sort of nod towards her. "We heard the news only a short while ago. It seems the Nazis ordered the police to round up many Jews in Paris, thousands of them, I'm afraid. They are being kept somewhere in Paris, near Paris anyway. You probably know the place, the *Vélodrome d'Hiver*. I think the same thing might happen here. The quicker you can get away the better. There are some terrible people in Lyon, in the police here, who would be only too pleased to have the opportunity to do the same thing. A lot of Jews have already left Lyon and the rest will go now if they can. Where did you say you were heading? Avignon, was it? Don't stay too long anywhere. Even the small cities will be affected. You should get out of France if you can, as soon as possible. I'm afraid there's going to be a catastrophe. Wait. I'll talk to my boss again. I'll see if I can get him to let you through straight away." He walked back to the kiosk.

"My God, Leon. What is happening to us?" Madeleine Cohn wailed. "My mother is an old woman. She won't be able to look after herself in some camp, or wherever they are being held. Maybe she was not taken. Perhaps she had already gone to Mme. Soubeyron's. She may be safe. Oh, my God! I must find out. I have to go back to Paris! I must try to telephone her."

"There won't be any public telephones," her husband told her. "We will have to wait until we get to Avignon. Perhaps we could drive a little longer today? It shouldn't take more than five or six hours from here. Yes. That's what we'll do. We'll get to my cousin's house tonight and telephone from there." He paused as the two officers appeared at the door of their bureau. They appeared to be arguing, the older man shaking his head as if he could not agree to whatever it was the younger man was saying. The younger officer used his hands a lot, in gestures which seemed to say "Be reasonable" or "Why not?". Eventually he put one hand on the shoulder of the older man and with the other gently withdrew the papers from his grasp. He walked unsmiling towards the Citroën holding the papers in front of him and thrust them at M. Cohn through the open window.

"Go!" he ordered them. "Get away quickly before he changes his mind. You might make Avignon before the curfew. I'm sorry we delayed you for so long. But go now as quickly as you can. Away from France. Free France we call it, but it is not free at all. Pétain and Laval are puppets of the Germans. They will do whatever the Nazis tell them to do, and that will be bad for you. What happened in Paris this morning will happen here before long. So go quickly."

"Thank you, Officer." M. Cohn's voice was husky. He coughed to clear his throat. "You have been very kind to us. Will there be any more roadblocks in Lyon?"

"No more in Lyon, but there should be blocks in all the main towns. Vienne, Valence, Montélimar, Orange. I don't know what to advise you. Just keep smiling and try to look confident. Wherever you go, go quickly and soon. I wish you well. Don't stop unless you must. You should make Avignon tonight."

"Thank you again, Officer. What is the time now?"

"It's almost midday. Almost midday on the sixteenth of July. I fear it is a day Paris will want to forget." He stood back from the car and waved them on vigorously. "Good luck!" he called as the car moved away.

"Can we not stop again, Papa?" Lucie said. "I don't like all these barriers and roadblocks and men in uniforms."

"That particular policeman in his uniform might have saved our lives," her mother pointed out, "but I agree with you. No policemen at all would be even better." She settled back into her seat as they left Lyon and the welcome shade of its long rows of plane trees and the river on their left, slower and more deliberate within the confines of its stone embankments, but like them heading south, to what it too might be hoping would be freedom. "At least I was right about the police in Free France," she said after a while. "They seem to be on our side down here, don't you think, Leon?"

M. Cohn nodded. "So far," he agreed.

They were not stopped in Vienne. The beautiful old town slept beside the Rhône as if its steep-sided valley was a bed, but near Condrieu a tyre was punctured and they lost almost an hour when they stopped to change the wheel. They crossed the river again to enter Valence, and skirted the city before turning south for the long straight run down to Montélimar. At Livron-sur-Drôme the solitary officer manning the main road was too lethargic in the brilliant heat of the late afternoon to bother with them and by six o'clock they were approaching Montélimar along a long undulating stretch of almost deserted highway. Alongside the road the Rhône rolled sluggish and grey between its reedy banks and beyond it rose the high bleak mountains of the Ardèche, sheltering the far side of the valley from the golden evening sun. A thin veil of cloud smeared the heavens to the south while across the river the beginnings of a flaming sunset threatened the cool blue of the sky.

The road into Montélimar ran directly towards the long granite hill known as the Plateau de Narbonne, crowned by the château of the Adhemar family from whom the town had taken its name. On the crest of the mountain the stone fortifications of the medieval castle were mellowed by the warm evening light, nestling almost surreptitiously in the blanket of dark trees, cedars and cypresses and mulberries and sycamores, which sheltered it.

On either side of the road orchards of ripening peaches and pears and apples stretched away in neat rows, almonds and pistachios hardened in the warm air and from the profusion of wildflowers and window-boxes came bees and wasps to mingle with the songbirds around the hives which stood in every field. Ahead lay the old market town, encircled by a wall of dilapidated mansions and shop fronts which separated it from the suburbs to the west, where newer, less graceful houses had spread across the broad flat banks of the two rivers flowing into each other's arms at the foot of the plateau.

An air of restfulness enveloped the Cohn family as they drove towards Montélimar, although they knew little enough about the place. For them it was still what it had always been, another town they had to pass through on the way to Avignon, a place they had seen several times in earlier, more peaceful summers, but there had never been cause to stop there, and in spite of its golden evening warmth and its fruit-scented air, to them, on this day, it was as strange as the moon.

At the end of the road as they approached the centre of the town, stood an arch of crumbling yellow stone, a folly in the style of the Romans, but erected hundreds of years after they had departed the area. For years it had caught the imagination of travellers coming down from the north, and now, at the end of this interminable, hot, troubling day, it seemed to Jean-Pierre like a sign they were entering a new part of France, a friendly southern region, distant from the cooler north, away from the frightening events of Paris and the border of the German sector. It was almost as if their dash for freedom had been successful at last.

The warm airs of Provence floated into the car through the hole in the windscreen, carrying the scents of thyme and sage and garlic and rosemary, and at the doors of cafés men stood about peacefully, smoking and watching their children tumble in the dust at the sides of the road. On rush-seated country chairs beneath the mulberries and plane trees which shaded the pavements, women sat in pairs or small groups, talking cheerily as if nothing at all could be wrong with the world, as if life in this part of France was perfectly normal.

"We must press on," M. Cohn said. "It's still at least two hours to Avignon, probably more. We should be able to make it tonight. They don't seem to be all that interested in us down here."

But he spoke too soon. From under the line of pleached trees which bordered the road a black-uniformed man stepped out, one gloved hand raised in a command to stop. Behind him stood two others, leaning against the open door of a car. One, a portly older man, looked at them without interest, the other, younger and insolent, rested a foot casually on the running board, a cigarette dangling from his fingers.

The Citroën came to a stop beneath the trees, and M. Cohn, feeling it was rather ridiculous with the shattered windscreen open to the road in front of him, rolled down his side window.

"Papers," demanded the officer who had stopped them. He glared at each of them in turn. Jean-Pierre thought he had the face of someone who might have been a bully at school.

Leon Cohn handed him the bundle of crumpled documents which had got them this far. Mme. Cohn leant across from her seat. "We are trying to get to Avignon tonight," she said. "We have something important to do there."

The man ignored her, inspecting their papers one by one, grunting softly or sniffing as he turned to each new document. When he had got to the last one he shuffled them carefully together again, rolled them into a tight bundle and replaced the elastic band around them as if to indicate that his business was over. But he did not hand the papers back to M. Cohn, he stood looking at the hole in the windscreen of the Citroën and at the occupants of the car as if trying to make up his mind what to do next. He poked the bundle of papers into the gaping hole made by the border guard and rattled it around, dislodging a few more pieces of broken glass. Then he motioned M. Cohn to get out of the car. A trio of passers-by stopped to stare.

"What is wrong, Officer?" Leon Cohn asked. "We had our papers inspected by the German guards at the border and then by the police in Lyon. They both let us through. What is wrong now?"

"The police in Lyon," mimicked the officer. "Really. The police in Lyon." He pulled himself upright, away from the car. "There is a militia nowadays in this part of France, M. Cohn. A militia which exists to deal with problems like you." He paused and glanced to one side as if to indicate that even the passers-by would be aware of the problems he was referring to.

"And I am pleased to tell you, M. Cohn, that I am not a policeman. My name is Desmarais. I am a Captain in the militia of Vichy France, and you, you and your family that is, are one of my problems." He withdrew the bundle of papers from the hole in the windscreen and tapped it on the bonnet of the car to remove any remaining splinters of glass.

"You nearly made it, didn't you?" he said. His smile was terrifying. "When did you leave Paris? Yesterday? The day before? You've done well, M. Leon Cohn, but I'm afraid you're not driving any further tonight." He took a pace back from the car and straightened his dark cap.

"Out!" he ordered. "All of you! Out, please." He waited until all four members of the family were standing by the side of the car, tired and nervous in their grimy clothes, before summoning his fellow officers from their watching place. "We've got four Jews here," he announced. "Came down from Paris in the last couple of days. That was good timing, wasn't it? Very good timing." He turned to Leon Cohn. "You must have been tipped off," he said with a sneer. "You must have friends in the right places who warned you what was going to happen, or you would have been picked up, like all the others who stayed in Paris."

"As a matter of fact," Madeleine Cohn told him, "we were thrown out of our apartment by the police just two days ago, acting on the instructions of the Nazis, I suppose, and we had nowhere else to go. That is why we are here. It had nothing to do with being warned to leave. We're not important enough to be warned of things like that. But now that we are here, perhaps you could help me? My mother is still in Paris and I need to speak to her. We won't be able to get to Avignon tonight and I must make contact with her. She's old and on her own in Paris. Would you mind helping me?"

The officer looked at Madeleine Cohn in mock amazement, before turning to his colleagues. "Do we want to track down the mother of this Jewess?" he asked them. He laughed harshly and there was a smile on his face as he waited for a response, but there was no reply.

"No, Mme. Cohn," he said, glaring at her and emphasizing her name, making it sound like an insult. "We cannot do anything for you. You deserted your mother, didn't you? If you were prepared to do that I don't see why I should try to help you now. We French don't do things like desert our parents. There is a custom we call family loyalty here, you know, but perhaps you people don't understand that?" He handed the bundle of documents to the plump officer behind him. "Follow me," he said to Leon Cohn, adding the word "please", as an afterthought. But it was an order, not an invitation.

"What about the car?" M. Cohn asked. "Where are we going?"

No one replied.

"We can't just walk away from it," M. Cohn said firmly. "Everything we have in the world is in the car. You can't expect us to leave it here."

"Stop whining at me," said Captain Desmarais. "You're not taking the car any further. You said you wanted to go to Avignon, so off you go. You can walk to Avignon. Nobody round here has petrol for a car any longer. Why should we permit you Jews to drive around in style? There are trains, buses, even a cart if your journey is essential. The car stays here. Now walk." He pulled a pistol from his belt, allowing it to swing gently from the index finger of his hand. "And I'm not waiting all evening either. Get a move on. That way. That's the way to Avignon." He pointed the barrel of the gun at them as they hesitated in the middle of the street. "Move!" he shouted.

They began to back away from him. Leon Cohn, with his hands guiding the children's shoulders so they were behind him, shielded by his body from the man's gun, his wife close to him, moving with him, but slowly, angrily, reluctant to walk.

Suddenly she stopped as if she had made up her mind about something. "No!" she announced. "No! I'm not going to walk. I'm a French citizen! I am entitled to my car and my possessions. I don't have to walk to Avignon or anywhere else. I am going back to the car, our car." She began to walk towards the dusty Citroën, stretching out a hand to it almost as if it was a mirage, as if by reaching it she would somehow be able to resolve all their problems.

The officer lifted his right arm, pointing the barrel of his pistol directly at her. "Stop," he ordered, in a firm measured voice. "Stop now, Madame, or I will shoot you."

Madeleine Cohn continued making her way to the car. She drew level with Captain Desmarais, only a few paces from him, and turned to look at him. "I am a French citizen, Monsieur. We are in Free France, and that is our car. There is no law which says I must walk away from our car, is there?" She smiled at the three officers.

She was still walking, still smiling, Lucie remembered later, as Desmarais fired a single shot into her head.

Her body crumpled to the ground as if it had been made of nothing but bubbles, as if in the instant of death her flesh and bones and muscle had vanished into thin air and only a bundle of clothes remained, lying in an untidy heap on the dusty road.

A cry like the moan of a waking child came from Leon Cohn's throat. He stood motionless, disbelieving his own eyes, his children behind him, peering out in terror at the corpse of their mother and the gun in the officer's hand.

The passers-by moved on quickly, muttering with embarrassed concern. For a few seconds the trees seemed to freeze, then, lifted by a breath of air, they resumed their shivering as the scent of smouldering rosemary leaves and scorched garlic drifted across from a nearby kitchen.

6.

Darkness was falling as they sat on a wooden bench in a small park which lay a short distance from the road to the south. M. Cohn rocked back and forth in silence, his arms folded across his lap, his head collapsed on to his forearms as if there was not an ounce of energy left in his body. From time to time he would raise himself up and feel for the hands of his children, but his eyes remained closed and he could say nothing to them. They huddled close to him like new-born lambs trying to attract the attention of a foster mother.

"Madeleine," Leon Cohn murmured. "Madeleine." He began again repeating his wife's name as though he had just remembered it. "Madeleine, Madeleine, Madeleine." Two hours had elapsed since he had seen her body taken off in the clattering truck and he had said nothing since then but her name, over and over again.

"She is dead, Papa," said Jean-Pierre, coldly. There was enough anger in his voice for a lifetime, anger at everyone, everything; at the militia, at his father, at Montélimar which at first had seemed so welcoming, at France which had disowned them, at God who had deserted them, at everything, even the weather-beaten bench on which they sat and from which they must start their lives again. "Maman is dead. Stop saying her name."

"Madeleine," M. Cohn repeated as Lucie leant against him, then, looking down at her as if he had only just realized she was there, he encircled her clumsily with his arm and kissed the top of her head, letting his lips rest for a while on her hair. Jean-Pierre, seeing that for the first time his father had recognized something other than his own grief, stood to face him. Neither wanted to be the first to speak. They stared numbly into each other's reddened eyes. It was almost night. The sun had glided off in a blaze of flame beyond the mountains of the Ardèche, drawing across the sky a few wisps of cloud glowing like embers to remind the town of the day it had given them.

"What are we waiting for, Papa?" asked Jean-Pierre. "What are we going to do?"

"I don't know yet," Leon Cohn said. "We must go somewhere. They ordered us to leave, but I can't believe they mean us to go, to leave Madeleine tonight. We don't even know where she is, or what they are going to do with her. I think I heard one of the militiamen whisper to me to stay, that he would come back to help us, but it's getting late. I don't think he will come now." He doubled over again, resuming his crouching position, but after a second he sat upright as if collecting his thoughts while his son looked up at him, thankful that at last his father seemed to be doing something. For almost two hours they had sat there, M. Cohn rocking backwards and forwards and crying softly, trying to muffle his sobs as his children looked to him for comfort, Lucie beside him numb with grief, clasping her hands together and forcing her knuckles into her eyes. Only Jean-Pierre was dry-faced, uncomprehending, mute with hopelessness, with the knowledge that his father had stood there seeing it all happen and done nothing. The boy wanted to leave, to run from his family and block from his mind his father's uselessness and inaction, to see none of them again.

But at last Leon Cohn stirred and collected his thoughts. He put an arm around each of his children, pulling them close to his own body and, together, as darkness descended on the park, they sat, absorbing their grief in silence, until the sound of footsteps on the stone path disturbed them.

"Don't speak," a man's voice whispered. He stood a few paces away with his back to them, speaking over his shoulder. "I'm very sorry for what happened this evening but now you must hide. New orders came in this evening from Vichy. You are in great danger. You must follow me. Quickly, please."

Leon Cohn recognized the plump outline of the older militiaman who had witnessed the shooting. "Stay behind me," the voice continued. "Not too close. As far behind as possible without losing sight of me. There is a bridge about three hundred metres from here. Near the bridge someone else will take over from me, someone who will look after you tonight. After that I don't know what will happen."

The man set off into the clear night. The moon had not yet appeared and there were no lights in the town. The three Cohns followed his indistinct shadow as he wound his way between the trees and slipped across an empty street before leading them to the high stone embankment of a shallow river. *Le Roubion*, said a sign pointing to it. The town could have been completely deserted. There could have been not another person alive. Not a vehicle moved. No lights shone from the windows of the houses which lined one side of their route. Only the plodding figure of the middle-aged man kept drawing them on, into the darkness, to a destination of which they knew nothing.

7.

They carried on past the point where the embankment ended and they could see the river Roubion itself, a narrow slow strip of water, shining in the light of the stars, but so shrivelled by the absence of rain that it did not flow so much as trickle across its wide gravel bed.

A bridge led off to their right, but the figure they were following kept on, turning if anything slightly to the left towards the foot of the rock plateau on whose crown perched the shadowy castle. They continued up a narrow street overhung on both sides by blank-faced houses, shuttered and barred against the night, and it was only at the first bend in the street, when the figure of their guide was silhouetted against the pale wall of a large house, that both children noticed they were no longer being led by the figure of the portly man. Instead a slimmer outline was ahead of them, walking more easily up the hill, which had become steeper, and stopping every few metres to look behind at them, making sure they were still following.

They lost sight of their new guide as the road took a sharp turn to the left, but as soon as they had rounded the bend they saw him again, no longer walking, but standing at the door to the large house, one hand outstretched to grip the door handle and the other beckoning them on urgently up the hill.

They stepped down from the street into an airy, unlit room with a stone floor. Their guide closed the door behind them, holding a warning finger to his lips. A dull light filled the room from a large archway open to a garden. Beyond the arch was a terrace and a pond, above which fireflies bobbed like marionettes. Further away, a row of plane trees drooped with the weight of their summer foliage, moths and bats flitted to and fro in the nightshade beneath the trees and from the branches of an ancient laurel doves called across the glassy surface of the pond.

"There's a light," whispered the figure of their guide, removing a beret to release a shower of golden hair. An oil lamp stood on a table to one side and in a few seconds it was burning feebly, casting no more than a glow on the walls of the room, but sufficient to show them the figure and face of a woman about the same age as Madeleine Cohn. She stood before them with her hands clasped in front of her as if unsure what to do next.

"I can't tell you much," she said. "My husband would have come but there was something else he had to do tonight. I have prepared some food for you." She spoke quickly as if there were many things she should remember and wanted to get them all said before she forgot them. "It's not really enough for three," she continued, "but I had no warning you were coming." She looked out through the arched doorway where the moths and fireflies danced. The doves continued their cooing and the leaves on the plane trees fluttered. At some other time, on some other occasion, it might have been a perfect night.

"I'm so sorry, Monsieur," she said finally. "I can't imagine how you are feeling. Nor you," she added, looking at Jean-Pierre and Lucie who stood motionless, stunned by the tranquillity of the room and the garden. "I'm so sorry for what happened today. I can't believe such a thing could have taken place in Montélimar." She raised a clenched fist to her mouth, unsure of herself. "Do you believe in prayer, M. Cohn?" she asked. "If you believe in prayer you might be comforted to know many of us have already prayed..." Her voice trailed off. It was something she could not explain.

Leon Cohn nodded. "I do believe in prayer," he whispered. "I hope prayer will be enough."

"There will be enough prayer," said the woman. "Come with me. You will sleep here tonight, maybe for a little longer, while we decide how to get you away. I'll show you a room. There is a room for all three of you. I thought after today you would want to be together." She led the way up a flight of stone stairs and along a passageway into another part of the house. "There's a sort of bathroom there." She pointed in the half darkness at a white-painted door. "You can drink the water from the taps, and I've made up beds in here. There are more blankets if you need them, but it's a warm night." Lucie shivered and the woman put out a hand to the girl's forehead. "I'll get an extra one for you now," she said.

"My husband will be here soon. He will explain what can be done for you. I don't need to tell you how important it is to remain quiet. Your bedroom is right above the road and a patrol passes this way every hour or so. Luckily the garden is very private. Tomorrow you might be able to spend some time outside if you stay close to the house, but you must move on very soon. It is too dangerous to stay here.

"Only yesterday the authorities started rounding up Jews in Paris and sending them away, God knows to where. And now there are rumours that Laval has offered to co-operate with the Nazis, that he and Pétain have agreed to do the same down here. We don't know when they are going to start, but my husband says Laval has agreed to send up to the northern sector any Jews he can find in Vichy France. They'll know you are still here, that you didn't go on to Avignon, and they will search for you. Even children will be sent away. For everyone's sake you must be very careful.

"Stay here for now and I will bring you your food to this room. We will not use the dining room, anybody coming to the door from the garden can see straight into it. When my husband gets back he will come to you if it is not too late. I will not see you again until the morning."

She backed away slowly, a troubled expression on her face and pulled the door shut behind her. In the last moments before they were lost to her view she saw the girl fall sobbing into her father's arms and for several minutes the woman stood alone in the dark passageway, unable to see for the tears which, try as she might, she could not keep from her eyes.

Leon Cohn was not a man who bore hatred. His life had not been without conflict, but he had always been able to forgive the few enemies he had made, or forget the differences which had caused the enmity. But on his first night in the house in Montélimar M. Cohn did not expect to sleep well. He felt his pulse racing as if he had run up a flight of stairs or climbed a steep hill. His hands were clammy with cold sweat and his body shook with fear and remorse, and something new, an emotion unfamiliar to him, an overwhelming anger at all those who had turned against him. Not just the particular policeman who had killed his wife, but all those who had forced them into leaving their apartment, and Paris, all those who had disrupted, and were now destroying, their lives.

In spite of his anger he did not wish for any revenge except to escape, to go with his children away from France. He wanted to run, not fight, but still his anger lurked and lurched within him, strangely alien in his gentle heart. He looked about him at the room in an attempt to distract himself, to focus on something else. A shabbily-curtained window over-looked the courtyard below them and a battered walnut armoire stood against the blank wall which fronted on to the street. In the centre of the room was a low round table on which a single candle burned. Three crude beds set hap-hazardly around the room completed the sparse furnishings. But still his mind raced.

They picked without enthusiasm at the frugal supper the woman had brought them, then pushed it to one side. They pulled all three beds in the room together so they could reach for each other during the night and they lay down fully clothed. Jean-Pierre and Lucie sobbed themselves to sleep a few minutes after their father had arranged the blankets over them, but for Leon Cohn the night was interminable. Twice he heard voices outside in the street below them, the voices of men, police he assumed since no one else was permitted to be on the street during the curfew, and for much of the rest of the night he tried unsuccessfully to blot from his mind the image of his wife falling to the road, her dress crumpling about her body, and afterwards the stillness, the silence, the absolute finality of it. The anger in him subsided to impotence and the impotence in turn swelled to a black despair which even his drowsiness could not dispel.

8.

Four people, three adults and a boy, stood before a pair of rusted iron gates which clung precariously to two pillars of crumbling stone. The gates had been twisted out of shape so that they could not be shut properly and they had been drawn together by a tangled length of chain and a padlock which looked as if it had not been unlocked for years. Dry grass from several summers had grown up around the gateposts and daisies climbed eagerly from it, stretching their small white and yellow faces upwards to catch the last of the day's sunlight.

Mme. Vigier, the oldest member of the party, rested her hand on the chain and turned to M. Benoit. "I thought we should approach the house from this side today," she said, in her bossy way. "Through the garden. We could enter by the street door if we wished, but I always find the view from the drive so pretty late in the afternoon."

M. Benoit did not appear enthusiastic at the prospect of walking so far, but his wife smiled at Mme. Vigier. "Yes, of course we can," she agreed. "I've never walked up the drive before. We will get a much better look at the garden, too. Come on, Oliver. You lead the way." They took turns to duck under the padlocked chain and squeeze through the narrow gap between the two gates.

The driveway looked as if it had once been well-maintained. From the gates to the first bend it climbed up from the road between two walls of plastered stone to each of which clung the remains of a straggling grapevine. A couple of fig trees stood at the turn and above them a tall Cyprus, wild-limbed and lop-sided, looked as if it might fall at any minute across what could still be seen of the path.

The bend was marked by a second, much more impressive gateway, not visible from the road. There were two more stone pillars, taller than the first pair, three or four metres tall, Oliver guessed, with a wide arch of spiked wrought iron above them and a plaque in its centre on which some words, long worn down, had been stamped. Beneath the arch was another pair of iron gates, partly open and very heavy, impossible to move, surrounded and hemmed in by stunted bushes and impenetrable mounds of briars.

The three members of the Benoit family stood below the arch, staring up at the metal plaque, trying to decipher the faint signs it bore. Mme. Vigier allowed them a few seconds before giving them the answer. "Le Bouton d'Or," she announced, "1856. That's the name of the house and the date it was rebuilt."

"I thought you said it was much older than that," Oliver complained to his father. "You said it was hundreds of years old."

"The oldest part is," M. Benoit replied. "Some of it must be six or seven hundred years old, but it has been rebuilt a few times. This sign was put up the last time it was done. In 1856. So most of the house you're going to see now is more than one hundred and thirty years old."

Mme. Vigier scowled knowledgeably as if she too could have told Oliver all that. She reached out, pretending to be playful, and gripped his scalp with all the fingers of one hand, tousling his hair roughly as if she would have liked to punish him. Then she began to move on. "Now, if you do buy this house," she said, "you will find the garden very rewarding. A lot of work was put into it when the house was built and all the planting was properly thought out. At one time it was the finest garden in Montélimar." She pointed to an overgrown thorn hedge and some dark laurel bushes to her right. "Those are very old," she said. "You won't get that sort of thing with a new house. And further on there are all sorts of nice things. I'll show you when we get closer. Oh!" She let out a little grunt of pain as she stubbed her toe on a stone hidden in the grass. "Perhaps the locals are right about this place." She bent to rub her foot. "Perhaps it is unlucky. I think I've cut myself." Then, in rather a hurry and in what she hoped was a soothing tone, she tried to correct herself. "What am I saying?" She laughed. "Unlucky? I must be mad. Not this place. No, not Le Bouton d'Or. It's absolutely delightful, as you can all see."

"My husband said the squatters are still here." Mme. Benoit was cautious about raising the subject. Mme. Vigier had snapped at her several times before for asking impertinent questions. It was the fifth house they had seen that afternoon, it was late in the day and they were all tired.

The estate agent put her hands on her hips defiantly and stood knee-deep in the long grass of the drive to face them. "There *were* squatters, my dear Mme. Benoit," she said. "There *were* squatters, but we have had them removed by the police. They will not be returning, I can assure you." She bent to rub her foot again. She wore light summer sandals and her toe was sore. "We should move on," she said crossly. "It'll be getting dark in a few minutes and we want to get a good look at the house while we can. And the whole garden, too. You're going to just love the garden. I can see you like it already, Oliver, don't you?"

Oliver didn't know how she could see whether or not he liked the garden, but he couldn't think of a reply so he pretended to look very hard at the light of the sunset ahead of him and he kept his eye out for squatters.

They walked on round another sharp bend where the drive traversed the face of a steep hill before passing into a thickly wooded area. Ancient oaks and chestnuts had shed the leaves of many autumns in a brown sea all around them. Small invisible creatures slithered across the rustling foliage and the roosting birds fell silent at their approach. Laurel trees and thickets of acacia formed a suffocating tunnel through which they passed, no grass grew beneath the dense, shady canopy above them and the ground under their feet was hard and dry. It seemed to Oliver they would never come to the house when suddenly the tunnel ended and they were once again in clean open air. Ahead of them stretched the driveway and, standing, almost hiding in the bushes at its side, were two children, no bigger than himself, Oliver thought, and about his own age too. He slowed and looked at them, but they were indistinct, almost invisible, as if they knew they had been seen and were trying to hide. Squatters, he thought to himself, and he glanced back to see if anyone else had seen them.

But his parents were busy admiring the garden and Mme. Vigier had stopped and bent to hold a piece of paper tissue to her sore toe. When she stood up she inspected it closely and Oliver, directly ahead of her, could see several small blotches of blood on it. "As a matter of fact," he said. "I really do like this garden. I don't even mind that there are squatters here. At least I'll have some friends."

"You'll change your tune, young man," his father said, "as soon as they steal your bicycle."

"Why should they have to steal it though?" he asked. "If they're going to be my friends I'll let them borrow it." He wished his father didn't always feel so strongly about things, didn't always expect people to steal or trespass or get in the way. He shook his head. He had hoped that things might change when they left England, that his parents would be happy to be back in France, especially with his father no longer caught up with his job at the bank.

"The bank, the bank." M. Benoit used to talk about it all the time. "I'll have to be at the bank early tomorrow," he would say. Or, "I have to go into the bank on Saturday." And when he was not talking about his work he would talk of houses or cars or clothes or furniture, always about possessions; of not damaging things, of never lending things or losing things, even old things like last year's anorak or a tennis racquet which could hardly be damaged anyway.

Oliver began to walk on, narrowing his eyes and hoping to see the two children again, but there was no sign of them, not even the crackle of feet on dry leaves. "It's my bicycle anyway," he muttered, "and I'll lend it to whoever I want."

To their left a stand of bamboo, disturbed by a gentle gust of wind, seemed almost to shudder with relief, while to their right, from the bank of the hill above them, pine trees dripped their pungent perfume into the soft evening air. At the side of the drive, late irises glowed blue in the fading light and, as they reached the spot where the children had stood, the scent of roses came to them from a bush entwined around yet another set of gateposts which marked the end of their walk. Oliver turned and scanned the garden. The two children had vanished without trace.

The house lay before them at last, a flat-faced three-storeyed building of warm golden stone and many windows. Too many, Oliver thought. The house was too big. Somehow he had expected it to be overpowered by the vast wild garden, and, indeed, at its base it did seem to be fighting to survive; creepers and vines and small twisted shrubs and trees swarmed all around it, reaching up to its walls with clamouring, devouring arms as if its presence offended them. But the house stood tall and aloof. It owned the garden. It was not afraid of it.

"Come on," ordered Mme. Vigier. "I will describe the house to you when we're inside." The final set of gates led on to a courtyard on a level with the middle floor of the house. A broad-limbed plane tree dominated the terrace, its branches stretching out to touch the two wings of the building which were joined at a right angle, forming two of the three sides of the courtyard. Below, four more plane trees marked the edge of a lower terrace in which Oliver could just make out the shape of a pond, "a trefoil basin," Mme. Vigier called it proudly, in the centre of which stood a stone plinth bearing a bronze statue of a small boy holding a trout to his breast. Water trickled weakly from the mouth of the fish, falling noiselessly into the pond in an intermittent stream of sparkling droplets.

"You should be able to get the fountain going again

properly without difficulty,'' said Mme. Vigier. ''It used to work by gravity. It was fed from a spring in the hillside so there was no pump needed. The spring is still there. You might have seen the stone tunnel leading to it. We passed it as we came up the drive. The pipes need some cleaning I suppose, but it's nothing serious, I'll tell you all about the garden later, oh, and about the golden dome, of course.'' She stopped and turned to face the courtyard again. ''Everybody thinks Le Bouton d'Or means golden button,'' she said, ''but in this case it means golden dome.

''The man who did all the work on the house back in 1856 had been a soldier in Algeria. When he came back to France he wanted something to remind him of the Muslim country he had left, so he built that funny little tower there, above the third side of the courtyard, with two tiny rooms in it, one above the other and a sort of minaret on top, completely covered in gold they say, when it was new. There, you can just see the outline, covered in creepers. It's a complete ruin now. You'll probably have to demolish it. Then you can give the house a new name if you like.'' She let out a harsh laugh and started off again.

''We should look around inside before it gets dark. There's no electricity, as I told you, and of course the house does need a little work. It has been unoccupied for a long time, quite a lot longer than you've lived, young man.'' She made as if she wanted to emphasize her point by grabbing Oliver's head again, but this time he ducked away from her outstretched claw. Disappointed, she led the way through the rose-bound pillars of the last gates and walked to the front door taking a key from her bag. She fiddled at the lock without success for a few seconds, then, shaking her head, she placed her hand against one of the heavy panels of the door. To her surprise it swung open easily, revealing a wide hall off which ran several other rooms and a cold, stone staircase.

"Oh. Yes," Mme. Vigier exclaimed, stepping inside and beckoning them to follow, as if the unexpected opening of the door was just what she had planned. She began to talk again, too loudly Oliver thought, as if she was trying to be overheard, as if there might be people in the house. "We will start with the salons," she said, opening the door to their left. "There are two on this level."

They followed her into the first of the two rooms. It was a frightful sight. There was rubbish everywhere, piled high in the centre of the room and in smaller heaps at the sides and in all the corners. Old sticks of furniture lay smashed on top of rotting mattresses from which the stuffing oozed in dry streams. Floorboards had been ripped up and windows torn from their surrounds. Picture frames had been wrenched to pieces and broken glass was everywhere. Against one wall a pair of wooden skis stood at a steep angle, a pair of sand shoes wedged into the bindings as if someone unfamiliar with winter sports had attempted a bizarre experiment.

Mme. Benoit wrinkled her nose. "It didn't seem as bad as this the last time I was here," she said. "It's absolutely frightful. I really don't think I could ever live here. And I'm sure there are rats."

"Of course there will be a few rats." Mme. Vigier looked quite indignant. "We're on the edge of a town, the house is unoccupied, there is a large garden, badly overgrown." She scowled as if the condition of the garden was somehow the fault of Mme. Benoit. "I've never seen any rats myself, but really, you've got to expect them in a place like this. You will be getting some cats, won't you, or a terrier?"

"I don't like cats," said Mme. Benoit. "It's not important. I thought I heard a noise, that's all. I thought it might be rats." She stopped and turned her ear to the ceiling. They all heard it this time, a shuffling noise as if something was being dragged along the floor above them.

"I can hear something as well," M. Benoit said.

"Me too," added Oliver quietly, although he didn't think it sounded all that frightening.

"Well, there you are," Mme. Vigier admitted. "There's probably a rat or two up there. Let's move on." She took one or two steps forward, carefully kicking some loose pieces of wood out of her way with her good foot. Then she stopped again and they all heard it, first the shuffling, then a tremendous howl. It was a noise which could not possibly have been made by a rat or any other animal. It was the roar of a wretched, disturbed man, a madman, then the raised voices of others, several men and a woman, two women perhaps, some of the voices bellowing loudly, others screaming as if a terrible fight was taking place. There was a violent thumping on the floor and the sound of running feet. Footsteps rang out on the stone stairway and finally, through the doorway to the hall, they could see the cause of the din. Several people came charging, howling and screaming down the stairs and into the hall. All except two ran or stumbled directly out into the courtyard and down to the garden, but one, a heavily-built young man and another, older and wilder looking, stopped and stared through the open doorway to the salon.

Mme. Vigier and the Benoit family stood transfixed with fright, with nothing between them and the unruly intruders but a large pile of rubbish. Mme. Vigier was equal to the occasion. She coughed, to clear her throat or perhaps to give herself confidence. "You've no right to be here," she said loudly. "This house is private property. I'm the agent selling it. I'll report you to the police as soon as I get back to my office."

The younger of the two men stared back at her insolently for a long time before he spoke. "Yeah?" he said. His voice was coarse and thick and loud. "And what if I tell you I'm staying?" His clothes were ragged. It looked to Oliver as if he had slept in them, and his shoes were tied with lengths of unmatched string. His hair was long and greasy and even from a distance Oliver thought he could smell him, smell the stench of the food and wine spilt on his clothing, the matted hair and the grime of his blackened fingernails. His gums seemed red and swollen and his teeth gleamed like a wolf's in the gloomy light.

Instinctively, Oliver moved to his father's side.

"Don't cause any trouble," said M. Benoit. "We're looking at the house, that's all. We'd like to look around in peace, if you don't mind."

"Sure," said the man. "You can look around my house as often as you like. I'll leave you to it. I was just going out anyway. Wasn't I, Jacques?" He turned to the other man.

"Yeah," agreed his companion. "We're going out for a while. Make yourselves at home. Be our guests." He laughed wildly. Then, like old friends, each threw an arm around the other's shoulder and they stepped back, still laughing, out through the open front door. Oliver walked to a window. For a second or two he could make out their shapes before they disappeared into the twilight, slipping like wild animals, he thought, down a flight of steps to the lower terrace and into the shadows of the low trees and bushes crowding in around the pond.

He re-joined his parents. "Is it safe?" he whispered to his father. "Will they come back?"

Mme. Vigier was ready with an answer. "They'll be easy to get rid of if you buy the house," she said. "The police will move them out in no time. Anyway, they're quite harmless. Drinkers, that's what they are. They wouldn't hurt anyone. They're probably more afraid of us than we are of them." She seemed quite confident of her opinion as she led the way up the stairs.

"The children didn't seem like that," Oliver said. "They seemed quite shy. They disappeared as soon as they saw us."

"They weren't children, Oliver," said Mme. Benoit. "They were grown-ups."

"No, the two on the drive," Oliver explained. "They were my age. The boy looked about thirteen and the girl a bit less, I suppose. They weren't grown-ups, anyway."

"It doesn't make any difference with squatters, Oliver," M. Benoit broke in. "Squatters, gypsies, whatever they are, they're all thieves, all dishonest. We want nothing to do with them, do you hear?" He cleared his throat as if to say that that was that. "Now, come on. Let's look at this house, shall we? Before it's completely dark."

Before them a door stood open to a large room with three long windows. From wall to wall the floor was covered with old blankets and cushions and pieces of cloth and sacking. Piles of newspapers lay around as if awaiting use and an assortment of rudimentary cooking utensils were scattered about the room together with some short lengths of sawn timber, a few broken branches and other items of fuel. The remains of an open fire smouldered on a square of corrugated iron set in the centre of the floor and wisps of steam rose from an old-fashioned cauldron in which a sort of stew was being prepared.

"If they're not got out of here soon there won't be any house left to buy," said Mme. Benoit. "Look at that. The boards under that metal must be almost on fire." She bent to pick up a plank, poking it at the iron square beneath the flames, moving it away to reveal the blackened timbers beneath it. "Such a beautiful parquet floor, too," she said sadly. "That will have to be replaced."

Mme. Vigier ignored her, moving on to the next room, but Oliver found himself fascinated by the human life outside the house. He moved to a window. A ghostly half-light had settled on the terrace and it took some time for his eyes to adjust to the pale glow of the moon beginning to fill the garden. Bats fluttered between the trees and moths fanned the air with their wings. Some kind of lizard with a transparent body clung to the one pane of glass still unbroken in the window. After a while he could make out the shapes of the squatters among the bushes surrounding the basin. Some were lying down on the dry grass or sitting with their backs against the stone steps or the trunks of the larger trees. Others walked about slowly, looking up at the house from time to time and muttering quietly. He could see the glow of cigarettes when they inhaled and occasionally the gleam of moonlight reflected on a glass bottle raised to thirsty lips.

There seemed to be more of them than he had noticed at first. He tried to count, but some of them were moving about and in the darkness he could not keep track of those he had counted. The two children were there as well, he noticed, although they did not seem to be part of the main group. They sat together at one end of the pond, away from the others, away from the edge of the terrace where the light was brightest. There was the boy, Oliver saw, and the girl a couple of years younger, eleven or twelve perhaps. They seemed hardly to know the others, yet they must surely be the children of the squatters. Why else would they be there? For a while he stared at them, willing them to look up at him, but they seemed engrossed in each other's company, paying no attention to anything or anybody around them.

He was woken from his wonderings by the harsh voice of Mme. Vigier, coming from below him outside the front door. "Come on, young man, unless you want to stay the night." His parents were beside her, his mother holding her arms up to him as if he might jump and his father smiling. Mme. Vigier had bent over to dab at her injured foot again, this time with a handkerchief. When she straightened up he could just make out a large, dark bloodstain on the soft white cloth. He could hardly stop himself from grinning.

"Wait!" he yelled, and turning, ran down the stairs and out through the front door into the night.

Even Mme. Vigier seemed to want to be close to his parents as they made their way towards the first set of gates where the terrace led on to the drive. Oliver, nearest the stone balustrades at the edge of the terrace, glanced over at the squatters. The adults had emerged from the shadows and were standing out in the open, their cigarettes and bottles clearly visible as they awaited the departure of the intruders. The two children were nowhere to be seen.

M. Benoit hurried on, his wife and son beside him. Mme. Vigier was last out through the gates, but they could all hear the sound of unhurried footsteps and quiet voices as the squatters made their way up the steps from the lower terrace and back into the house.

They walked away steadily as the tunnel of bay and laurel closed over their heads. Oliver was the only one to look back. The fire had flared into life again. He could see the flickering of flames on the walls of the room on the top floor and the shadows and outlines of the men and women as they moved to and fro across the open windows. And there too, at a lower window, towards the far end of the house, he could make out the figures of the two children, standing very close together, holding hands perhaps and looking, he was certain, directly at him.

9.

If it had been left to Oliver Benoit he would not have chosen to live in Le Bouton d'Or. They had looked at many nicer houses around Montélimar, he thought, some with swimming pools, one with a tennis court and several with gardens and tall trees for climbing, and none of them had been taken over by squatters either. But his parents liked the size of Le Bouton d'Or. Mme. Benoit was particularly fond of the terraced garden and the way all the windows looked across the valley away from the town. It was almost, she said, as if the house was in the country, yet she could still walk to the shops and the markets. She might run it as a guest house, she said. It would make a perfect guest house, and now M. Benoit no longer worked in London, they wanted to start a small business in France.

No one ever referred to the fact that M. Benoit had lost his job at the bank. Oliver knew it had happened, that that was why he had been taken away from boarding school in England. Such an expensive school too, his father always used to say, while Oliver's mother pretended nothing had changed. But M. Benoit was still angry about it. "I'm still a young man," he would complain. "Forty-five next year, and I'd done a lot of good work for the bank, too." He was still unable to accept that he, François Benoit, a director for seven years, had been told suddenly, without warning, that his job no longer existed. He could go back to Paris, to the office there if he wished, they had said, but he had refused that offer. He would rather be his own man, he said, start a business perhaps, and yes, in France, why not in France, where he knew everyone, where he had grown up and gone to school.

Mme. Benoit had been more than willing to leave London. She had always liked the south of France, particularly the area around Montélimar. Her only fear was the squatters. She hoped they would be frightened off as soon as work began on the house and in order to ease her mind her husband promised to change all the locks on the doors and asked the police again to clear the vagabonds from the property.

No one really believed that new door-locks would make any difference, virtually every window in the house could still be climbed through without difficulty, but M. Benoit said it would have a psychological effect. It would make the intruders realize that a new owner would be moving in soon and they would have to find somewhere else to squat next winter.

But it was not only the locks which needed changing. *Everything* needed to be done to the house. There were long meetings with builders and plumbers, carpenters and electricians, stonemasons and painters, until eventually M. Benoit was satisfied that work could start.

They rented a small house in a nearby village while the work of restoring the house was being carried out, close enough for M. and Mme. Benoit to visit Le Bouton d'Or every day to supervise the builders. Oliver would join them sometimes, but usually on Sundays when he was not at school, only rarely on the days when the house rang with the sounds of Claude the electrician drilling, or Laurent the plumber sawing pipes and chiselling channels into the walls.

At the end of each visit M. Benoit would ask the workmen

the same question. "Any sign of the squatters today?" he would say, and invariably he would receive the same answer.

"Not a sign of the grown-ups, M. Benoit," would come the reply. "We've seen the end of them, but those kids are still hanging around. They still appear from time to time."

"But they belong to the squatters, don't they?" M. Benoit asked, the third or fourth time this conversation was repeated. "If the squatters have gone what are their children still doing here? Can't you frighten them off? I don't want to go to the police again over a couple of kids."

"Maybe they weren't with the squatters," Oliver suggested. It was a Wednesday and he had the afternoon off school. "Perhaps they live near here. They might be neighbours. Please don't frighten them away. Please. I might like them."

"They're squatters all right," said Claude. "No doubt about that. Did you see their clothes? Normal kids don't wear clothes like that. Some of their things must be years old, funny shoes, long socks, little short trousers on the boy. My lad wouldn't be seen dead in that sort of thing. No, they're squatters. Cheeky little devils too, still hanging around after their parents have moved on." He took up his drill and placed the shining steel bit against the wall to show that that was that, the conversation was over. M. Benoit shook his head to indicate that he knew Claude was right but that he wished he wasn't.

Oliver tried to look out of the nearest window into the garden but he didn't want to let anybody know he was hoping to see the two children, nor that he was hoping they might see him again. He knew what his father would say.

After two weeks he was still not enjoying his new school and he would have liked to find some new friends close to home. He could speak French quite well, although his English was better, but there were so many differences, so many new rules and so much homework. He longed to be back at school in England. He had enjoyed boarding. It was better for an only child and he had had a lot of good friends there. He missed playing football too, and nobody at his new school knew anything about the English teams. In France all they seemed to want to do was stand around the playground at lunch time discussing songs and singers he had never heard of. He was not one of them. He longed for five o'clock and the solitude of the bus journey home.

But as the months passed he became used to the idea of living in Le Bouton d'Or and in his quiet way he was looking forward to it. He built in his mind a picture of the two children from the garden and he would day-dream of the adventures they might have together after he moved into the house. The trees they could climb, the shaded paths along which they could bicycle, the basin in which to swim and set their sailing boats and the secret rooms in the old wing of the house which they could make their own, where they could have their private conversations.

At first his imaginings were all of the house as it was during the long warm days of summer, but the work on the house seemed to take for ever. It was mid-winter before it was ready for the Benoit family and by then Oliver was sure the children would have long departed to join their parents, wherever they had gone after leaving Le Bouton d'Or.

10.

The Benoit family began moving their furniture into the house on a weekend in late January when wreaths of snow lay on all the hills around the valley and dense clouds hung threateningly over the town as though daring its inhabitants to hope that the cold weather might lift. The air felt thin and brittle and hard as if it had blown from the farthest reaches of the Arctic and it held the trees and gardens of Le Bouton d'Or in a grip so intense it seemed as if life itself had stopped.

No birds sang, no lizards scurried across the stone walls, no mice twitched their noses at the daylight. A layer of ice several inches thick covered the surface of the basin and in it, imprisoned in the clear frozen water, the goldfish waited for the thaw, curled into extravagant shapes like autumn leaves set as decorations in a glass bowl.

Oliver had chosen a bedroom on the top floor of the house which overlooked the courtyard and the lower terrace with its pond. During the summer, when the plane tree had been in leaf, the room had been shaded and cool, but now, to his delight, only the tree's bare leafless limbs stretched up beyond his window, allowing the feeble sunlight to enter the room and warm the skin of his face and hands.

He opened the window to look at the removal men working below him. A truck stood in the centre of the courtyard. From its rear door a pair of thick wooden planks leading to the front of the house served as an unloading ramp. The workmen were walking purposefully to and from the truck to the door of the house wheeling cardboard cartons or packages on trolleys. Sometimes two or three of them appeared at a time, weighed down with heavier pieces of furniture which they handled more slowly. Some of the cartons were labelled "Crystal. Fragile" or "Ornaments. This way up", which they handled delicately. Others said simply "Clothing" or "Kitchenware" which they tossed about as if they were of no importance at all. It was going to take all day at least, Oliver realized, to empty the first truck, and there was another, further down the drive, waiting to be unloaded when the first was finished.

He shifted his gaze to the lower terrace, to the goldfish. He began to count them, using his fingers and starting with the closest of the three arms of the basin. He had got to forty when he was distracted by a movement to one side of the pond, but he continued counting until all five fingers of his left hand were down before he directed his concentration from the fish.

He shook his head, annoyed at having allowed himself to be distracted. Nothing was moving but the gently waving branch of a bay tree and beyond it, on the high stone wall, a few sprigs of dull green ivy shaking limply in the frozen air.

He looked back to the fish in the pond. He had memorized the point he had reached and began counting again immediately. He got to fifty-four before he noticed the movement once more. This time he stopped counting straight away and stood up sharply, leaning out of the window, staring intently at the dense foliage of the bay tree. There was something there, something behind the tree, and it was moving, but the tree was thick and overgrown with a multitude of suckers at its base making it almost impossible to see through it to whatever was behind it.

For several seconds Oliver did not move, did not take his eyes from the tree and then, sensing that he in turn was being watched, he stepped slowly back from the window, as far back as possible into his room without losing his view of the terrace, until the morning sun was no longer lighting his face or his body. He remained perfectly still, invisible he hoped, as he waited.

The next movement he saw came not from behind the bay tree but from further away, almost at the far end of the lower terrace, where a palm tree rose unexpectedly from a clump of briars on which ivy had taken a hold. This time he could see clearly what had moved. It was the smaller of the two children of the squatters, the girl, and she was returning his gaze, almost fearlessly he noticed.

Oliver stepped back towards the window, resting both hands on the sill to give himself an air of authority. He was searching for words when he saw the boy emerge from the shelter of the bay tree. He too stood still, in full view of the house, apparently unafraid. He looked up at Oliver staring down at him, then walked slowly, almost casually across to the girl, his sister perhaps, and stood beside her, so close their hands were touching.

"You," called Oliver, in a voice less confident than he'd intended. He stepped back to the open window. "You! What are you doing?" The two children stared back at him as if he had not spoken, as if they had not heard a sound. He called again, louder this time. "Who are you? What are you doing here? Where do you live?"

He saw the girl move her hand nervously and the boy take it in his own as if to reassure her. They seemed to have none of the boldness Oliver had noticed in the older squatters. He thought they seemed frightened of him rather than the other way round.

"Stay there!" he ordered. "I'm coming down." He withdrew his head from outside the window and began to turn towards the door of his room when he noticed that they too began to turn away. He paused, keeping his eyes on them and called again: "Don't go! Please. I'm coming!"

He raced down the two flights of steps to the lower floor of the house and grasped the handle of the inner doors. It turned easily and he pulled the doors open. The shutters were next. It was an awkward handle which needed to be lifted, then turned and pulled at the same time. He struggled with it, perhaps for five seconds before it gave and he could push the shutters apart. He half fell out on to the terrace, his eyes scanning the bushes for the two children, but he was too late. They were nowhere to be seen.

He ran to the spot where they had stood together, then to the bay tree where the boy had first appeared. He clambered up the stone steps to the courtyard, but there was only the open truck and a solitary removal man, resting with a cigarette in his hand. He ran back down and searched the bushes surrounding the pond, but the pair had vanished. There were no children to be seen anywhere.

His father's head appeared at a window and his mother called from a balcony. "What are you doing, Oliver? Have you sorted out your room yet? Come on. There's such a lot to do. You've no time to be playing about down there."

"I saw the children again!" he shouted. "The squatters' children. They were here, just a minute ago. I came down to talk to them, but they've disappeared. I can't understand it. Where can have they gone to?"

"You shouldn't have gone down to them, Oliver," M. Benoit said. "I don't want you being friendly with them. I want them to go away. You're not to encourage them to stay around the house. If we're not careful we'll have their parents back as well, and if that happens we might as well forget about having the place to ourselves. If you see them again just ignore them, or call me and I'll send them packing. Now come inside and finish putting away your things."

Oliver walked slowly up the steps to the front door and into the house. He was angry. His father knew nothing about the two children, they had done nothing wrong, yet he was forbidden even to speak to them. He did not want the children to go away. They might be the children of squatters, he thought, but they did not look unfriendly, they looked quiet and shy, frightened almost. Not the sort of children who would make a mess of a house, or steal things. He was angry with his father for wanting to frighten them off, angry that he had been taken away from all his old friends, from the school he liked and brought to France where he knew no one, and angrier still that here in his own garden were two children his own age and he was forbidden to have anything to do with them.

That night was the last night he slept in the village house. A wind had got up in the early part of the evening and blew all night, driving the cold winter air in through the gaps around the windows of his bedroom and sending the curtains billowing and shivering away from the walls and fluttering up towards the darkness of the ceiling. Oliver pulled the duvet over his head and clutched his hot water bottle to his chest, thinking of the two children by the frozen pond in the garden of Le Bouton d'Or. They would have gone by now, of course, but where to? And who with? Where were their parents, and where would they sleep tonight?

He fell asleep still thinking of them, but when he dreamed it was of other things. He dreamed of his school in England and his friends there. He dreamed of football and the house they had lived in on the edge of London, the only house he had known since he could first remember, with its neat lawns and beds of rosebushes, of the tree-house his father had built for him years before and the swing made from an old tyre and a heavy rope slung from a wide flat branch of the tallest tree in the garden. He dreamed of the smell of pine needles which used to cling to his shoes and socks every time he had played on the swing and finally he dreamed again of his school friends and the games they had played, the fun they had had together.

He was lonely. Now, lying alone in his room, he wished they were moving back to London rather than to the strange old house in France with its huge empty spaces and its secretive gardens.

11.

By the afternoon of the following day, Sunday, their move was complete. The Benoit family now lived in Montélimar, at the house called Le Bouton d'Or, and on Monday Oliver Benoit walked to school as if nothing had changed.

Some of the other children had begun to talk to him as if he was a member of their gang. One, Philippe, the most popular boy in the class, had sat next to him at lunch one day, but Oliver still felt a strangeness with them, as if he was different, or they were. Few of them showed any interest in his life outside school and even they did not seem to have any time to listen to the stories about the house and its pond and trees, or the squatters and their strange children in the garden. For his part Oliver was no longer worried that he was not joining in all the weekend activities the other boys talked of each Monday morning. Already he had begun to believe that he would make his friends elsewhere.

He told himself he was content to walk home alone, and to be alone. In the first months of that winter his weekends were spent helping his parents in the house or clearing under-growth and fallen trees from the drive with his father. Several times as they worked together M. Benoit said how pleased he was that the squatters seemed to have taken themselves off at last and how relieved he was that they had not stayed and caused trouble. He seemed to assume that his son agreed with him on the subject since there was never any discussion of the matter, but not only did Oliver not agree with his father about the squatters, he was not at all sure they had gone, at least not the children.

Twice he had seen them down by the pond and once, early in the morning, he had taken them by surprise, much closer to the house, directly beneath his bedroom window.

He had knocked on the glass pane, firmly, but not so loudly as to frighten them, and they had heard him too, for they had looked up, but they had not replied. He had had to lower the curtain in order to free his hands to undo the window catch and in the instant his view was blocked they had disappeared.

Once, after a particularly cold night, he had begun to search the garden to see if there was a hiding place at the foot of a tree or below one of the stone walls where they might be able to shelter from the winter mistral, somewhere they might store food, a blanket or two perhaps, or warmer clothes to keep out the biting cold air. But he had found nothing, not even a pile of dry leaves on which a pair of young heads could have lain. It was all a mystery.

Even their clothes puzzled him. Oliver recalled the electrician's conversation with his father about the little short trousers on the boy and how old-fashioned they were. The girl too, on the three or four occasions he had seen her, was also strangely dressed. She wore a light cotton skirt or dress with a pretty pattern of small red flowers on it and an unusual pair of sandals which fastened with a buckle across her instep. They were the sort of shoes Oliver had worn when he was a toddler, not the sort of thing a girl of eleven or twelve would wear, even if she was the child of poor parents.

And stranger still was that every time he had seen the pair they had been wearing the same clothes. It did not seem to matter whether it was early in the morning or the middle of the day, whether the sun was shining or the iciest of gales was blowing, they always wore the same things: the boy a pair of grey short trousers, long woollen socks and black shoes and a white cotton shirt beneath a dark blue jersey and his sister (Oliver had never doubted they were brother and sister) the cotton dress with the pattern of flowers on it and a red cardigan. On her feet were short white socks and the same pair of old-fashioned sandals.

It was all very puzzling, Oliver thought, very strange, but stranger still, strangest of all, was that they never seemed to feel the cold, nor even to be aware of it. He often wondered about that, especially when he lay in bed at night with the mistral howling across the roof of the house and gusting down the chimneys, hammering at the shutters and doors and rattling the windows in their frames.

He had begun to leave his bedroom shutters open in order to be able to see out at night or in the early mornings and sometimes, when a particularly vicious wind was blowing, he would throw off his bedclothes and creep to the window, gazing out at the storm-tossed garden, hoping for a glimpse of the children, or even sometimes wishing he would not see them, hoping they were somewhere safe and warm. They rarely showed themselves, however, and Oliver began to tire of keeping vigil for them until one dreadful night in early March, a Friday night.

A mistral had begun earlier in the week, slicing through the streets of Montélimar like an icy knife, blowing the Wednesday market stalls into disarray and hurling grime and sodden leaves into the faces of the shoppers. It continued for three days. Tiles were ripped from the roofs of houses, loose doors were torn from their hinges and trees were uprooted or, if their roots were stronger, simply stripped of their branches.

The garden of Le Bouton d'Or suffered too, but less than most, lying as it did in the lee of the hill and the old château which dominated the town. For three nights the noise of the wind kept Oliver awake, until on the Friday night, with a clear sky and a full moon, when it reached its frightening crescendo, he could stand it no longer.

It was almost midnight when he stood at the window. The four plane trees on the terrace below him shook wildly, their bare spindly branches waving as loosely as if they were threads of string. The palm trees swayed dangerously, their fronds snapping angrily in the air like whips, and further away from the house the two giant cedars, the tallest trees in the garden and less sheltered than the rest, bent southwards, like huge prehistoric animals hunching their shivering backs to the dreadful wind. But there was no sign of the children.

Oliver stood for several minutes scanning the courtyard and the terrace and the moonlit garden stretching into the distance. Eventually, disappointed, he turned away, to stand beside the old cast-iron radiator his mother had insisted on keeping in his room. He leant back on it to warm his legs and hands. He was almost asleep on his feet, his eyes half shut, when he noticed a movement against the far wall of his room. An old sofa stood there, beside an umbrella stand in which he kept his tennis racquet and fishing rods and a butterfly net he had never used which his uncle had given him for Christmas a few years earlier. At first he thought something must have slipped, the net perhaps, but he knew that sort of movement would have been accompanied by a noise and no sound had come from the umbrella stand. He stood perfectly still as his eyes, fixed firmly on the sofa, adjusted to the darkness of the room and he could see more clearly.

Then he saw it again, another movement, something was there. He felt his scalp tighten and a shiver at the back of his neck. He held his breath noiselessly, trying to back away towards the door leading to the hallway. His hands touched the wall behind him and as he spread his fingers to meet the familiar rough plaster he heard, from somewhere near the sofa, a cough, a child's cough, and then he saw them quite clearly, first the girl in her familiar white dress, then the boy, her brother, taking her hand in his. Their eyes were fixed firmly on Oliver, who stood speechless, not so much with fright as with amazement that the children should choose such a time to show themselves to him, and in his own bedroom as well.

12.

Somehow he had always known they were waiting for him, that they would come to him one day, but still, for a few seconds he was unable to talk, and when he spoke his voice was less friendly than he would have wished.

He had planned to tell them his name and ask theirs in turn, but all he could say, sounding rather like his father he thought, was, "What are you doing in here, in my bedroom?"

There was no answer. The girl lowered her eyes and drew a long slow breath. The boy stared into Oliver's face, looking as if he wanted to speak but could think of nothing to say.

Oliver spoke again, this time using the words he had originally intended them to hear. "My name is Oliver," he said quietly. "This is my bedroom." He paused, wondering how they had got in. He had been at the window for only a short time and he had not heard a door open. "When did you come in?" he asked. "You shouldn't be here you know. My father doesn't want you in the house any more. You'll have to be careful. I keep seeing you in the garden but I'm not allowed to play with you and anyway you always disappear just when I think I can get to you."

The boy put his hand to his mouth as if he was about to clear his throat and speak, but then he seemed to change his mind and he lowered it again almost immediately.

"Where do you come from?" Oliver asked. "Do you sleep in our garden? I thought your parents had gone away. Why are you still here?"

The boy moved his hand again, but this time he spoke, shyly and with his fingers almost to his lips as if to hide his words. "Those people are not our parents," he said. "They've only been here a few years. They're nothing to do with us." He had an odd voice, Oliver thought, rather formal, like a grown-up's voice, but he spoke very clearly, not like some of the children at school with their strong Midi accents.

. The little girl raised her eyes to Oliver's. "We've never spoken to those people," she said. "Our father told us not to speak to anyone, and we haven't until tonight, not since he went away."

"Where has he gone? Your father, I mean," asked Oliver. "And what did you mean about those people, the squatters, having been here only a few years? How long have you been here?"

The boy shook his head as if he did not want to reply, but the girl squeezed his hand to give him confidence. "We don't know where our father is," the boy said at last, "and there has been nobody we could ask, not since," he paused, rubbing his eyelids angrily, "not since he left us here."

"When did he leave you?" Oliver demanded. "And where did he go? What are your names? People don't just go off leaving their children by themselves. When did this happen?" He was angry now. They looked like nice children. Too nice and too young to have been deserted here in Le Bouton d'Or, alone in the garden, in winter too. They could become his friends. How dare their father simply go away leaving them, he thought, with no one to look after them.

"You can call me Alain," the boy replied, "and you can call my sister Marie."

The girl almost smiled and added, "And our father told us we should say our family name was Bouchet, but those are not our proper names." Her brother looked sharply at her, but she held her chin higher and continued. "Papa told us not to use our real names because they would give us away if the police heard them."

"What do you mean, if the police heard them? What have you done?" Oliver was beginning to wonder if the children were quite as nice as he had thought at first. "Why should you need to change your names?"

"We haven't done anything!" the boy snapped back quickly at him. "The police were against us but we haven't done anything. They came looking for us but they didn't find us."

"Well you must have done something wrong," Oliver said. He had no idea what the boy was talking about, but he assumed he was lying to him or hiding the truth. There must have been something they had done and now wished they hadn't. He stared at them in bewilderment for a while. Neither child gave any sign of wishing to answer him. They simply looked at each other and then back at him, saying nothing, their faces expressionless. "Well," he continued, beginning to sound angry again. "If you won't tell me I can't help you. And you still haven't told me what you're doing here, in my house."

"It was our house too, once," said Marie. "Only for a few days, and a long time ago, but Le Bouton d'Or was our house, too. We never really left it. We've been here all the time."

13.

The dawn brought birdsong and sunlight and the warm scent of early morning grasses flooding into the room. Reflections of green leaves dappled the walls through the shutters and the doves, which had not ceased their cooing until after midnight, began again, like small, heavily-muffled church bells.

A man sat on a chair by the window, almost invisible with the light behind him. He put a finger to his lips as he saw M. Cohn stir and he beckoned him. Leon Cohn slipped off the end of the bed so as not to disturb his children and followed him from the room. The man led the way to a kitchen in the basement of the house. He turned when he reached a table in the centre of the room and held out his hand.

"You can call me Paul," he said. "It's not my name, but I don't want you to know my name nor even the name of this house or its address. You'll understand the reasons for that. I know your name, of course, M. Leon Cohn."

Cohn raised his eyes in a question, then, realizing the policeman who had helped them would have known his name from their papers, he took the other's hand. "I can't ever thank you," he said. "I've no money, nothing. Everything we had was in the car." He looked down at the clothes he had slept in. "This is all I have in the world." He shrugged and spread his hands helplessly before him.

"There is bread here," the man told him, "and a sort of coffee. We've got used to it by now, but I'm afraid it isn't very nice. And we don't have sugar any more either, but there is some raspberry jam from last year, when we still had sugar. Will you have breakfast with me?"

"Your wife was very kind to us last night," Leon Cohn said. "Much more than kind, in fact. I feel guilty that you are putting yourselves in such danger on our behalf. I suppose the punishment for helping Jews on the run is quite severe."

"It is not severe yet," the man told him, "as it has been a crime only since yesterday, but I expect soon it will be very severe. That's why we must get you away as quickly as possible. Where were you heading when you were stopped?"

"Avignon."

"Well, we won't be sending you to Avignon. Our organization is stronger in Toulouse, that's where you must make for, but I might as well warn you it won't be easy with two children."

Leon Cohn shook his head. "I won't go without them," he said. "How could I after what happened yesterday? To their mother, I mean. I don't think they would let me out of their sight."

The man nodded in agreement. "I know that," he said, "and I'm so terribly sorry about your wife. It has shamed all of us here. But I'm not asking you to leave the children behind. I'm simply telling you it will be more difficult to travel with them."

Leon Cohn studied the man who called himself Paul as he moved around the kitchen. He was about his own age, perhaps a little younger, in his early thirties. He was tall and well-built, with the powerful body of an athlete or a manual worker, but his hands were graceful, even as he was engaged in ordinary things such as handing a plate or pulling a cup from a shelf, he moved with the easy elegance of an animal, sure of himself, sure of every movement of his limbs. He had short sandy hair and a moustache, his blue northern eyes were patient, almost serene.

The woman entered the room behind Leon Cohn. She smiled at him as he turned, holding out an egg in one hand and a white plate in the other on which were a dozen or so strawberries, still wet with dew. "For breakfast," she said. She kissed her husband on the cheek and busied herself at the wood-stove. Cohn feared he was about to cry again. She was young, young and beautiful like Madeleine had been. It was more than he could bear to see her with her husband.

"I must check the children," he announced. He pushed back his chair and almost ran from the kitchen. But they lay asleep still, Jean-Pierre with his sheets wound tightly around his body as if he had been bound in them, and Lucie huddled in a tiny ball under the blankets, as motionless as an animal in hibernation.

He made his way back to the kitchen. The man was sitting at the table with a map spread in front of him. He glanced up at M. Cohn and patted the seat of the chair beside him. "Come and look at this," he said. Leon Cohn sat down. The man pointed to the map. "The only way is west," he said. "You must get across the river and then on to Toulouse, but through the small towns, Alès and Millau I think, then Albi. There is too much activity in the Rhône Valley so you must go west. You will have to cross the Rhône as far upstream as possible, starting from Ancone and crossing to Le Teil, then you must go down the west bank towards Bourg-St-Andéol. I will prepare a map for you. There are some reliable people in

Bourg. If you can get that far they can take you to Alès, then you can go on to Millau through the mountains with another guide. But you will have to come with me tonight so I can show you where we keep our boat and how to get past Rochemaure to Le Teil. That will be dangerous, for both of us. And there is another problem. My wife has to go away just for the night, so there will be no one here to look after your children. They will have to stay here alone tonight. She must leave this afternoon.''

Leon Cohn began to protest. "But I can't leave my children here alone," he said, "after all they've been through, their mother, yesterday. . ." His voice trailed off as the other man placed a hand on his arm. "Listen to me," said Paul. "You must allow me to organize this. My group is going to risk the lives of quite a few people to get you and your children to Toulouse. Either you put yourselves in our hands completely or we can do nothing for you.'' He smiled, he was not unfriendly, but Leon Cohn knew there could be no argument.

"What must I do?" he asked.

"The children can be hidden here tonight, not in the house, that would be too dangerous with my wife and me away, and the police know we are not living here any more so any noise or movement would be suspicious. But there is a sort of tower in the garden, I will show you later today. It is rather inaccessible and it cannot be seen from the town. Even if the police come to the house while we are away they would never think of looking in the tower. We will put the children in there with food and water and plenty of blankets and I will lock it so no one can get in. It's absolutely safe, and we will be gone for less than twelve hours. Even if we are delayed, my wife will be back tomorrow afternoon. And the weather looks settled," he added. "They can come to no harm. Go now and see if they are awake yet."

Cohn walked back to the room where his children lay. For a long time he stood at the door gazing down at the beds in which they had passed the night. Jean-Pierre stirred in his sleep, rubbing his hands in his eyes and rolling over with a sigh which seemed almost peaceful. He might have been at home in the apartment in Paris. Lucie's body moved too, but in a slow, even series of almost imperceptible movements, like the breathing of a cat in sunshine. It took some time before Leon Cohn heard the strangled sobs coming from beneath her blankets. She was awake and crying. He sat down beside the tiny mound her body made beneath the rough bedclothes and let his hand rest on it.

"There isn't any way we can forget what happened yesterday," he began. "I can hardly believe it myself, but if you want to talk about it now I will talk about it with you."

"No!" Lucie shouted. She threw the blankets off her and sprang up to a kneeling position on the bed. "I don't want to talk about it! It didn't happen, it didn't happen! It was a dream, Papa, wasn't it? It's not true, is it? She is not dead!"

"It is true, Lucie. Maman has gone. She won't be coming back. I wish it wasn't true but it is true, and there is no point in pretending. I can imagine how you feel, I know how I feel. It's as if something inside me, some huge part of my body has been torn out of me and thrown away. I feel such a pain there, such an emptiness, knowing she won't ever come back, and I need to tell you this, to share the pain with you. There is nobody in the world we can talk to now you know, except

ourselves, and we must talk about it. This pain won't go away
unless we talk about it. I know this is true.''

Jean-Pierre turned over in his bed. His eyes were wide open
and he looked steadily at his father. "She shouldn't have been
the one to die," he said. "Why was it her who tried to go back
to the car? It should have been you, not our mother, not a
woman.''

M. Cohn swallowed hard, only too aware of the accusation
his son was making. "She was always a brave person, Jean-
Pierre, and she was brave yesterday. We all saw that.''

"So why did you let her be the brave one? Why didn't *you*
try to keep our car? You did nothing! You just stood there!''
The boy's hard eyes never left his father's face.

"What would you have liked me to do? I am different from
your mother, Jean-Pierre. I am not the sort of person who
ignores the orders of a man who is pointing a gun at me. Is
that what you wanted me to do?''

Jean-Pierre shook his head angrily. "She's dead, that's all I
know! And she shouldn't be dead. She should be with us!'' He
fell back on to his bed, weeping and thrashing his legs about,
his hands spread white-knuckled on the hard straw-filled
mattress while his father looked at him helplessly.

"Come and eat breakfast," said M. Cohn finally. "We have
got to make plans today and none of us can think on an empty
stomach.''

14.

Later that day Paul sat facing Leon Cohn across the kitchen table. "I've received a message from my contact in Le Teil," he said, "on the other side of the river. He will meet all three of you there tomorrow night, at ten o'clock, and take you down to Bourg. Tonight I'll show you how to get across the river, and tomorrow, after dark, you'll be able to cross on your own, with the children." Paul took off his jacket and reached down to untie the laces of his heavy boots. It was late in the afternoon and he had been walking for almost two hours.

"The boat is about five kilometres away as the crow flies, just a bit up-river from Montélimar. We will have to leave the house here before the curfew begins. If we get there too early we will wait until dark, then I'll show you the boat and take you a little way out so you will be familiar with it. We'll take some rods and nets too, so we've got an excuse if anything goes wrong. There is almost no moon and plenty of shelter near the bank.

"I have arranged for the boat to be left for us near a little village called Ancone. It's well up from Le Teil so tomorrow you can go downstream with the current. Fortunately the water is not high at the moment and the river will be slow. You shouldn't have any problems getting across.

"Tonight, when we have finished, we'll sleep somewhere near Ancone, under a hedge I suppose, and we'll come back in the morning when the curfew has been lifted." He pulled off his boots and socks and massaged his toes, red and swollen from the afternoon's journey. He swigged water from a tin mug.

"And my children?" asked M. Cohn. He knew he had no choice but to go with Paul to see the boat, but he would have to explain his absence to Jean-Pierre and Lucie and he knew how fearful they would be at the prospect of being deserted, even if only for a few hours.

The children had spent the day in the courtyard outside the house, looking at the goldfish in the pond, and lying in the sun's warmth, their father sitting close by, watching them as intently as if he feared that by lifting his gaze for even a moment they might disappear from his view. The woman, Paul's wife, had been with them during the morning and early afternoon, but she had gone then, stooping to kiss each of them in turn as they stood by the pond, before turning abruptly and walking away.

"My husband will be back in an hour," she had said, "and everything is locked so no one without a key can get in or out from the street." She had waved a final farewell as she reached the door leading to the kitchen. "I'll be back tomorrow night, but you'll probably have gone by then. I wish you good luck."

She had left supper on the table, two loaves of stale bread, some withered olives and a lump of cheese. There was a simple salad too, and a bowl of apricots, and when Paul returned he produced a small jug of red wine, pouring most of it into the glass in front of M. Cohn. At seven o'clock they ate, the children silent and fearful, without appetites, eating only to please their father. As soon as they had finished they cleared away their plates and stood in an expectant cluster at the kitchen door. Paul picked up a basket from a dresser and lifted the clean white cloth covering its contents. There was a bottle of water and two mugs, some fruit and a few thick slices of bread. He delved into his pocket and produced a padlock and a key, he pointed to a bundle of blankets on a chair, motioning to M. Cohn to bring them.

They filed out of the kitchen and up the spiral stairway from the lower terrace, then across the courtyard to the foot of another flight of steps which wound up through a tunnel of wisteria and a cascade of white roses. At the top of the steps, or at least as far as they could see, as the steps wound round a corner and continued upwards, stood a small square-shaped tower crowned by a dome which marked the end of one side of the courtyard. From below, as they stared up at the place they knew was to be their hide-out, the children were able to make out traces of glistening paint on the surface of the dome. The colour was indistinct in the fading light, and so little of the paint remained on the chipping plaster that it was impossible to be certain, but Lucie imagined it might once have been covered in gold.

"Is that a part of the house?" she asked. "It looks strange, not like the rest of the building."

"It looks Turkish," said Jean-Pierre, "or Arabian. I like it. It looks like an Arab church. We were doing Algeria for history in school, before, when we were in Paris." He stopped suddenly. He had been trying not to remember anything of his past life, but back it all came. He dug his fingernails into the palms of his hands to hurt himself, to make himself forget.

"What is the name of this house?" he asked the man called Paul.

"I don't want to tell you that," the man replied. "You

shouldn't know anything about me or my wife or this house. You must forget everything about us and about Montélimar." He bent down to bring his face close to the children. "You could get us into trouble if you know too much, so, I'm sorry, but the house doesn't have a name."

"Well, we can give it a name, can't we?" Lucie asked. "A name we could think up ourselves. It's a nice house and the little tower up there is beautiful. Perhaps I could give a name just to that part of the house, the little Arabian part?"

"Yes. You can do that," said M. Cohn. "When we get back tomorrow morning you can tell us the name you have thought up. Now, we must get you settled in there. You have plenty of blankets and food, and you can't be heard from the street so you can even talk, very quietly of course, but if you hear anyone in the house or the garden you must be absolutely silent. You understand that, don't you? Not a word." He put a warning finger to his mouth.

They began to climb the first two flights of steps, rounding the turn until they could no longer see the house. The door to the lower of the two rooms stood ajar. Ancient cobwebs hung like shrouds across the walls and an old garden rake leant against one corner hemmed in by a collection of geraniums withering like skeletons in their earthenware pots. They continued on up the next flight and waited while Paul opened the wooden door into the upper of the two rooms.

It was a small square chamber less than two metres across and not high enough for a man to stand in, but it was clean and dry and filled with the scent of roses. There was a small triangular opening for a window at the top of one wall, big enough to take a large bird, but too small for a human, even a child, to get through. Leon Cohn spread the blankets on the floor and Paul put the basket down in one corner. On a ledge halfway up the wall was a candle in a blue enamel stick and a box of matches. "This is for emergencies only," Paul said. "If there is anyone in the courtyard below the light could be seen, so don't use the candle unless it is really necessary." He backed out through the low doorway and stood waiting, the padlock and key in his hand.

Leon Cohn knelt on the floor holding out his arms to Lucie. She took a step towards him and returned his embrace stiffly. "You are coming back, aren't you?" She looked anxiously at him, her eyes flitting backwards and forwards across his face as if to fix it in her memory.

"Why must we be locked in?" demanded Jean-Pierre.

"We are not locking you in to keep you in, but to keep others out and it's only for a few hours. It's to protect you. Really it is. Paul knows what could go wrong if anyone discovers you, don't you, Paul?"

The other man nodded.

"It's the only way we can keep you safe," Cohn continued, "and of course we will come back as early as possible tomorrow morning," he reassured them. "The curfew is lifted at six o'clock and we will start back then. We should be here no later than seven or seven-thirty." Lucie tightened her grip around her father and he felt the dampness of her tears on his neck. "And this is to remind you of your mother and me," he added, holding up a tall-stemmed rosebud the colour of a fiery sunset. "For both of you, until I come back." He laid the half-opened flower on the ledge beside the candle. "Perhaps you can put it in your water mug for a while tonight, to keep it fresh.

"And you have your big brother to look after you," her father went on. He slowly lowered his daughter's arms to her sides and reached out to his son. "I know what you think about yesterday, Jean-Pierre," he said. "I wish you felt differently about me, but today is today, not yesterday, and I must go. You understand, don't you? I am not leaving you. I'm coming back and then we will go away together, away from France."

Jean-Pierre stared over his father's shoulder out through the open doorway.

"Do you know what I thought about last night?" M. Cohn continued. "I didn't sleep at all. I lay awake thinking how brave your mother was, and you my son, and Lucie too, but all in different ways and at different times. None of us has any idea how brave we will be able to be until the circumstances arise. You will see that, when the time comes.

"And never forget what your mother told us. We are remarkable people, we Cohns. All of us. The remarkable Cohns."

Jean-Pierre did not reply. He stood with his hands by his sides, as his father knelt to face him. The boy's whole body was rigid, he stood like a soldier at attention, unsmiling. "I liked the way my mother was brave," he said at last.

"So did I," said his father. "She was a wonderful woman." He waited, his hands reaching up to his son's taut body, but there was no embrace, no sign of forgiveness. "Please kiss me, Jean-Pierre," he whispered. "I don't want us to part like this." The boy leaned forward slightly and allowed his cheek to rest for a moment on his father's temple, but there was no warmth in the gesture.

Leon Cohn got to his feet. "Goodnight," he said. "I will see you both in the morning." He bent to pass through the doorway, and turned when he was outside. "I love you both," he said. He looked intently into the room, but it was growing dark and he could barely see their faces.

After the two men had gone Lucie poured a little water into one of the mugs and placed the rose in it. It seemed to glow as bright as a candle and in a few minutes by its imagined light she fell asleep.

15.

The man who called himself Paul took a last look around at
the kitchen before stepping outside into the garden. He
locked the door and turned to Leon Cohn standing beside
him in a pair of country shoes and a suit of drab clothes the
woman had produced for him. It was half-past eight. The
evening, heavy and warm and dark, had begun to settle on
Montélimar and in the half hour before the curfew would
empty the streets, the people of the town were making use of
what was left of the day.

The two men mingled easily amongst the figures on the
pavements. If an observant policeman had been watching, he
might have noticed the pair walked more surely than the rest,
as if they were going somewhere rather than simply taking the
air, but they walked at a measured pace, they hesitated from
time to time, they stopped to light cigarettes and once or twice
Paul tossed a greeting to a familiar face outside a café. In a
quarter of an hour they were away from the town, in open
country, heading towards the Rhône, but north, to a place a
few kilometres from Montélimar, to the flat plain where the
village of Ancone lay close to the riverbank, surrounded by its
wheat fields and orchards, its vegetable gardens and a few
strips of vines.

By the time they came to the village the curfew was in force
and they skirted around the huddle of stone houses, slipping
along the edges of small fields, stumbling across walls or
clambering over gates, all the time watchful, listening, tipping

an ear to the sky or an eye to the land ahead of them as they made their way towards the smell of the river.

Once or twice a dog barked and a shout could be heard as its owner came to the door to quiet it. They found themselves sharing a field with six or seven lambs who bleated softly but made no effort to inspect the intruders. Drowsy geese hissed from a cage of wire and chickens gurgled in a shed, but there was nothing to hinder their progress. By ten o'clock they were standing on the eastern bank of the Rhône.

"We are looking for three mulberry trees," Paul whispered, "forming a triangle. There is a stream which joins the river here, and reeds all along the bank. Look where you are going or you will have wet feet for the night." He moved forward slowly, M. Cohn following as best he could in the darkness, convinced they were lost, that he would never be able to find his way alone. The waters of the river slid past them slowly, dense and heavy as a lava flow, but cold, the air above it sharp and thin after the fetid atmosphere of the town. Somewhere in the distance a train whistle shrieked.

"There they are," Paul whispered. He stopped and pointed to a clump of trees directly ahead of them. They continued on, crouching low to the ground, their shoes rustling the grasses and mosquitoes humming at their ears. A river bird called nervously and a brace of wild duck leapt into the air from the bank to their left, vanishing in an instant into the night. "There is the boat," he said. He took a few steps towards the river and came to a stop where a reed-filled inlet wound its way from the bank. A small dinghy lay half out of the water, its gunwales almost hidden in the wet-footed rushes, a rope leading from its bow to a stone anchor lying on the higher ground of the bank. Two oars were fixed in position in their rowlocks and an unlikely collection of rods and nets and bags was laid neatly beneath two planks which formed the seats. The vessel was ready.

"We'll only go a few hundred metres downstream tonight," Paul whispered, "enough for you to get the feel of the boat and so you will know your way after the Rochemaure bridge." They pulled the dinghy out through the reeds and climbed in, pointing its nose to the broad sweep of the river. Paul took up the oars and began to row. "You will want to get away from the eastern bank quickly," he said. "You have to pass beneath the bridge at Rochemaure and there are guards there sometimes. You'll need to be halfway across the river by then. We are lucky with the moon though, they'll hardly be able to see you even if they are looking, but you must be careful when you go under the bridge. It's quite narrow between the arches and you may be better to stop rowing in case you need to fend yourself off. This river can turn you in any direction, at the last minute too." He bent his shoulders and plunged the oars into the water.

In a couple of minutes he stopped rowing and held the dinghy steady in the water on its oars. "Look, there's the Rochemaure bridge. You can see it well enough from here, so we'll stop. Tomorrow night you'll go straight on through the central arch, then make your way towards the western bank. You've plenty of time. It's almost two kilometres from Rochemaure to Le Teil and just as you approach Le Teil the bank is low for a couple of hundred metres. Ground the boat there and my friend will be waiting. Don't go too far downriver, though. If you get as far as the bridge at Le Teil there is nowhere to land. So make sure you get close to the far bank and stop well before you reach the town."

"It will be fine tomorrow," Leon Cohn assured him. "It will all be downriver. I might need some help getting back now, but tomorrow I will be fine."

Paul dipped the oars into the water, turning the dinghy away from the dark outline of the bridge's central span until the blunt bow pointed upstream again. He passed an oar to his passenger, sitting at the stern of the boat. M. Cohn took it cautiously, judging its unfamiliar weight in his hands, deceived by the size of the river into thinking the boat was moving at no more than a slow walking pace.

A few seconds passed and the dinghy began to drift downstream again. "Come on," Paul whispered loudly. "You've got to take them both if you're to row properly." He held out the second oar as the boat began to turn and gather speed in the surging mid-stream water, but it was too late. The pillar of the Rochemaure bridge, so slim and fragile from a distance, suddenly loomed broad and threatening, directly ahead of them. Paul hissed a warning and Leon Cohn swung his oar to the side to fend them off, but the boat was travelling so fast that he was unable to get the blade past the pillar and the oar was dashed from his hands to splash behind him into the rolling water. The dinghy ground its wooden gunwhale noisily along the stone pillar of the bridge before drifting free.

"What's happened?" Paul demanded. "What are you doing? For God's sake, where is your oar?"

"I've dropped it," M. Cohn explained in confusion. He twisted around on the hard plank of his seat to look behind him. There was no sign of the oar. The dinghy carried on in the centre of the river, well past the Rochemaure bridge now and turning in a long slow circle in the swirling waters disturbed by the pillar.

"Sit still," Paul ordered. "We'll never find it in this light." He looked around anxiously as they drifted out of control, his eyes gauging the distance to the nearest bank, then sweeping the top of the bridge behind them for signs of alarm. But the speed of the river had already taken them beyond any danger from guards who might have been on the bridge. "Try to pull your seat up," he said. "If you can get it free we might be able to use it as an oar. I can't think of anything else. We've got to get ashore soon. We will never get through the next bridge, the one at Le Teil. It's netted. We'll be stuck there like fish until they haul us out in the morning."

It took two or three minutes to work the plank free from the screws which held it to the frame of the dinghy. M. Cohn could see the houses of Le Teil against the skyline as Paul drove the broad wooden seat into the water in a desperate effort to steer the boat through the currents in the centre of the river, but it was futile. Too much time had been lost. They went on serenely, almost majestically, carried far from the bank they had set off from by a long, slow bend in the river. When they were within shouting distance of the bridge at Le Teil, Paul spoke again.

"Can you swim?"

"Yes, I can swim."

"Good. We can't stay in the boat. We'll have to slip out here and head for the western bank."

Cohn began to protest. "But what about the children? We can't cross the river now, with no way of getting back!"

Paul dismissed his objection. "We're closer to the western bank now, so that's where we must go. Try not to splash. Come on. Now!" They tumbled overboard simultaneously, the dinghy somehow remaining upright. The cold, deep water of the river gripped their bodies as if it was a living thing, turning them around and over like leaves churned by a strong wind, and dragging at their clothes and heavy shoes. It was almost impossible to swim but somehow they made it, paddling like dogs to the steep-sided bank a short distance upriver from the bridge and clinging to it with desperate fingers, clawing at the weeds and stones which edged the river and lifting themselves hand over hand to the safety of the grassy embankment.

Leon Cohn lay face down, spread-eagled on the dry land, gasping for breath, his eyes shut. Somewhere nearby he could hear Paul groaning. "What is it?" he whispered. "Are you all right?"

"No. I hit my head on something, a rock, I suppose. I think it's bleeding."

"I'm coming."

For a few more seconds M. Cohn lay still, then he rolled over on to his back, his face upturned to the sky. The moon seemed to have emerged, he noticed, the light seeping in through his closed eyelids. He sat up, blinking. He heard a voice close to him, not Paul's voice, but another, unfriendly and harsh, a voice of authority questioning him. He opened his eyes. A torch was glaring into his face. He could see nothing behind it, but the voice continued and the toe of a heavy boot was prodding him to move. "Get up," the voice repeated several times. "Who are you and what are you doing here?"

He could see another torch nearby lighting the squatting figure of Paul and behind it a uniformed policeman, his other hand holding a truncheon or some kind of a weapon. "Are there any more of you?" the voice above him demanded.

Leon Cohn shook his head.

"Good. Let's go. Then you can tell us who you are and what you are doing here. I suppose you have your papers?"

"Where are you taking us?" Paul asked. His voice was slurred and feeble. "Come on, Officer. We are fishermen from up the river, from near Ancone. We lost an oar. Let us go back and find our boat. I know we were breaking the curfew but there is no moon tonight. It's perfect for fishing."

"Show us your papers, fisherman. Then you can go." The policeman with M. Cohn held out his free hand.

"My papers are at home," said M. Cohn. "I never bring them fishing. It's too risky."

"Say all that again, fisherman," demanded the policeman.

To the laughter of their captors, Leon Cohn repeated his words.

"With an accent like that," the policeman sneered when he had finished, "you expect us to believe you're from Ancone, a fisherman?"

"Come on." The other prodded Paul with his gun. "Let's go and find out who you really are. Your boat will be safe in the net. You can get it in the morning if you've been telling us the truth."

16.

Jean-Pierre was awake long before the songs of the birds sweetened the dawn air. He had burned with anger most of the night. His father had made him feel guilty by being so reasonable, so understanding, yet it had been his father who had not done anything to stop his mother being killed. He could never forgive him for that. For standing by as she walked to the Citroën, while the militia captain pointed his gun at her head and shot her. What were men for, he asked himself, husbands especially, if not to protect their wives? Now she was dead and his father was still alive. And then, last night, he had managed to make Jean-Pierre feel guilty for accusing him of doing nothing. It wasn't fair.

He sat up, a blanket wrapped around him. He didn't want to have a row with his father. Lucie hated rows and they had problems enough to worry about. He would keep his anger to himself for now. Lucie was still asleep. He would wait for her to wake before eating, although he was already hungry.

Through the small opening at the top of the wall facing him he glimpsed a sombre patch of clear western sky left over from the night. The sun had not yet risen fully but he could see no cloud. It would be another perfect day and soon they would be released from their cramped hideaway, able to leave Montélimar and its memories as they had left Paris, away from German border guards who seemed to hate them, away from French policemen who could do little to help them, and yes, he almost had to force himself to think about it again, away from Captain Desmarais of the militia of Vichy France who had shot his mother. He looked at his watch. It was a quarter to seven. He stretched across to the ledge on the wall to take the brilliant rose from the mug where his sister had put it. He cradled the bud in his hands and sat back, leaning against the wall and drawing the blanket closer round his shoulders as he tried to sleep again.

He must have dozed for more than an hour, for his sister was awake when he looked at her again, lying motionless on her blanket, her head resting on a tattered cushion, the curls of her hair flooding across it and on to the floor. She smiled at him, a smile of greeting from a sad face, he thought, but at least she had slept.

"Shall we have something to eat?" he asked. "I'm hungry. I couldn't eat last night."

"Yes." She sat up. "Me, too. What is there?" The white dress with its pattern of small red flowers was more crumpled than ever and dirty from the dust of the walls and floor of the room. The red cardigan was bunched uncomfortably on her shoulders as if she had put it on in a hurry.

"There's not much. Water and bread and some fruit. We'll probably have something else when Papa gets back." He looked at his watch again. "It's almost eight o'clock." He replaced the rose in its mug.

They ate most of the bread and all but two of the apricots. They drank water, sharing the other mug, although Lucie spilled some of hers and they finished the bottle pouring her a second mugful.

By half-past eight they had put away the basket and sat

waiting impatiently for the sound of footsteps in the courtyard or on the stairway.

"Perhaps they had to go further than they thought," suggested Jean-Pierre, "or they couldn't find the boat. It must be difficult getting about, with the curfew, I mean. I'm sure they'll arrive any minute. Listen." He turned his ear to the window as if he had heard an encouraging noise.

"I didn't hear anything," said Lucie. "What are we going to do?" She pulled the blanket up around her shoulders to comfort herself.

"There's not much we can do," Jean-Pierre pointed out. "We've got to stay here until they come back for us. Anyway, there is nobody in the house, or if there was somebody they wouldn't be on our side, would they? So there is no point in getting out of this room. We would just have to hide somewhere else. I'm going to try to sleep again."

By midday they were both worried. The garden hummed with the wings of busy insects and contented bees droned along the boughs of the weeping rose which tumbled around the domed tower and down into the courtyard. From further below they could hear the continuous plopping of water from the fountain in the centre of the pond, but there was not a sound from the house.

The children spent the afternoon dozing fitfully or, when they were awake, trembling with an exhausted fear. Even Jean-Pierre had begun to lose hope when at last they heard the sound of a door being opened. They sat up, brushing their hair from their foreheads and throwing off their blankets. It was almost five o'clock. They could even hear the sound of voices inside the house and below in the courtyard. They stood in readiness but they did not call out. The voices they could hear were unfamiliar, hard, angry voices, someone was giving orders, there were several people, all of them men, Jean-Pierre thought, and they seemed to be searching for something, or someone.

He put his finger to his lips, then motioned to his sister to sit. "They are policemen, I think," he whispered. "They might be looking for us."

"Some of them are in the garden," Lucie replied. "I think they are just down there, at the bottom of the steps." She hunched her shoulders and sunk her neck into them in the gesture her grandmother had used a few days earlier for the same purpose. "I don't like it," she said. "Where is Papa?"

"Shhh. Listen, they're talking. I can hear them." Jean-Pierre stood slowly to put his ear closer to the window. The smell of cigarette smoke drifted up and into the tiny room, bringing with it snatches of conversation.

"There's nothing here," said a voice. "We're wasting our time. Let's have a look around the garden. It's quite a place."

The children heard loud footsteps climbing the steps towards their hide-out. There was a rattle and a crash as someone entered the room below them, then the sound of heavy feet again climbing the next flight of steps. A hand fumbled with the padlock and the door shook as a boot tested its strength. "No," said the first voice. "Nobody's been through that door for years."

"Yeah," a second voice agreed. "There couldn't be anyone in there. What's the name of this place anyway?"

"Can't remember. That fellow in Le Teil said a name, but he told a pack of lies all night about everything else so why should he have been telling the truth about the name of the house?"

"So, what did he say it was called?"

"Something fancy. Something about gold, wasn't it? Yes. The Golden Dome. I think that's what he said it was."

"That's right. Le Bouton d'Or. Strange name for a house, isn't it?"

17.

The night Leon Cohn had spent at Le Bouton d'Or had seemed the worst night of his life. Nothing could blot from his memory the scene of his wife's death. He saw it over and over again, her defiant walk towards the car, the militiaman's raised arm holding the gun, the crack as he fired and then the slow, almost dreamlike fall of her body to the dusty street, while all the while he had been unable to move, helpless, useless, rooted to the ground beneath him. It had been worse than any nightmare because it had not been a nightmare. Every picture in his memory was true, unforgettable, stamped on him for ever.

But the night in the police station at Le Teil was no better.

They were hauled, Paul and he, into a small bare room and pushed up against the wall by the two policemen who had caught them. Their clothes were sodden and even in the warm night air they had both begun to shiver uncontrollably from the cold. One of their captors, the junior of the two, left the room.

"Papers! Papers! Show me your papers!" The words were hurled at them repeatedly by the remaining policeman until they had to answer.

"We have no papers," Paul said. "Our papers are at home, across the river in Ancone. We were fishing. Let us go home and we will bring our papers back here in the morning."

The policeman laughed. "Sit down," he said. He waited as they slumped to the floor, then he nudged Leon Cohn's ribs with the toe of his boot as he squatted against the base of the wall. "I don't believe this is a fisherman," he said. "Let's go through your story again, shall we?" He pulled up a chair for himself and settled into it.

"Now. You were in a boat. We know that's true, it's been spotted at the bridge, did I tell you that? A very small boat too, so we can assume you didn't come far. And you finished up on the west bank so we might also assume you had succeeded in crossing the river, mightn't we? But you had lost an oar, not the sort of thing a couple of experienced fishermen would do." He smiled, pleased with himself. "Nor were you carrying any papers." He paused as if reflecting on their predicament. "Of course, if you *had* been fishermen I might have believed that you didn't want to take your papers with you in the boat, but since we know you are not fishermen the fact that you did not bring your papers makes me suspicious. I wonder . . . I am wondering," he stared at the ceiling speaking quietly, as if he was talking to himself, before lowering his gaze suddenly to glare at them in triumph, "if perhaps you haven't come from Montélimar!"

"You," he poked his foot at Paul. "What's your name? You could be a local, but I'm not so interested in you, well, not yet anyway. However, *you*, my friend," he prodded Leon Cohn again, harder this time. "I think you are the fellow who was on his way to Avignon. We have been wondering where you had got to. My friend in Montélimar, my good friend Captain Desmarais of the militia, telephoned me earlier tonight. He told me he regrets letting you go. He says he should have kept you. Oh. By the way, I was sorry to hear about your wife."

Despite himself, Leon Cohn let out a cry at the mention of

Madeleine. He tried to struggle to his feet but the policeman leaned forward and rested the weight of his arms on the prisoner's shoulders, forcing him back down to the floor.

"So!" he boasted. "It looks as if we've got ourselves M. Leon Cohn from Paris, doesn't it? What timing, what perfect timing." There was a look of genuine pleasure on his face. "France wants as many of you as we can lay our hands on, you know. Did you hear that, M. Cohn from Paris? There is work for you now. We know you have been out of work for a while, but now there is plenty of work for all you Jews. We're getting you all together and offering you work. Laval sent word only this morning to all Vichy France. As many as possible, he said. Men, women, every one of you. Even children."

He released his grip on Cohn and stepped back. "Yes, children too, M. Cohn. Children too." He waited, his eyes searching his prisoner's face as if daring him to speak. "Where are they? Where are your children? A boy of thirteen, I hear. He should have a good few years of hard work in him. And a girl too, eleven, isn't she, or twelve? Yes, there will be plenty for her to do. Well! We need all the workers we can get, you know. France wants everyone to have work." He folded his arms across his chest and sat back, pleased with himself, pleased with the success he was making of his night's work.

"Perhaps your friend can tell us where your children are hiding?" He bent to look at Paul shivering on the floor, a pool of water oozing from his sodden clothes and spreading around him, the drops still running from his hair turning pink on his temple as they mingled with the blood from his wound.

"What is your name, friend of the Jew?" he asked. "What are you doing in such company? You might as well tell me.

Two officers of the militia are on their way here from Mon-télimar. They will recognize you, I'm sure. If you tell me now, perhaps I could make things easier for you. Otherwise I might think you are a Jew also and send you to Paris with your friend Cohn. And after Paris, who knows?" He paused, pleased with himself again. "Somewhere east I think, that's where all the jobs are, towards Russia, or Poland, if you're lucky. You could be there in time for winter. That would suit you, wouldn't it? You look as if you like the cold." He threw back his head and laughed, digging the toe of his boot into Paul's freezing body.

"Not speaking, eh? Well, we have plenty of time. It's just that, you understand, if I can find out who you are, without any help from the chaps in Montélimar, I'll get most of the credit, and that would be good for me. And what's good for me could be good for you also, don't you see?"

Paul dragged himself up to lean against the wall, his eyes never leaving the face of his captor. "My name is Paul Chaix," he said at last. "I'm not a local. I'm from Lyon."

"What are you doing this far from home?"

"I was on my way back from the south."

"Alone?"

"Yes. Alone."

"And what were you doing in Montélimar with this Jew?"

"We met in the park. I had already found a house to sleep in, an empty house. He came with me last night."

"But he was not alone last night. There would have been two children with him." The policeman was pleased with himself. He was finding holes in the prisoner's story already.

"There were no children. I didn't see any children. We

slept in a deserted house, and tonight we were planning to go our separate ways again. The main road over there is too busy." He nodded towards the east. "We wanted to cross the river. We had both lost our papers. We stole the boat somewhere near Ancone." He was looking more confident now, as he wiped a smear of blood from the side of his face. "We're nothing, Monsieur. You might as well let us go. I'm going to Lyon and Monsieur here is going south, I think. You've nothing to gain by holding us here any longer."

"Of course, M. Chaix. If your story is true, I'll probably let you go on your way. We will find out soon enough if you are telling the truth." He glanced at his watch. "Captain Desmarais from Montélimar should be here at any minute. We will wait." He settled back into his chair, but he had scarcely made himself comfortable before a bell rang in the outer office. He stood and left the room.

Leon Cohn turned to Paul in dismay. "What are you up to?" he whispered. "What about my children? We've got to tell him. We've got to tell him if we are to get them out."

"We can't do anything for your children while we are in this place. At least one of us has to get away, both I hope, if we are to help them. But I have to think of my friends too, my organization, my wife. If they discover who I am they may be able to destroy my whole group, and that won't be any good for others like you who need help. Anyway, if we don't make it back, my wife will. She'll be there tomorrow. She can let the children out. She will look after them."

Cohn knew the truth of Paul's words but he shook his head, unable to accept what was happening. They waited in silence.

In a few minutes they heard the sound of the key turning in

the lock and once more the door was opened. The policeman from Le Teil stood facing them, one hand resting on the brass handle of the door. Behind him were two officers in the uniform of the militia and all three were studying the faces of the prisoners slumped shivering against the wall.

"Ah, yes," said the taller of the new arrivals. He strolled into the small room, rubbing his hands together as if he were about to enjoy a festive meal. "We don't need any introductions at all. I know both these gentlemen. M. Cohn from Paris I met only yesterday." He turned to the police officer. "I think I told you of the unfortunate incident with the woman who tried to escape, didn't I? And you." He fixed Paul with a threatening smile. "What is it you are calling yourself tonight? M. Chaix, I hear? M. Paul Chaix, is it?"

He laughed merrily. "We are old friends, aren't we, M. Chaix?" He bent low in a sort of bow, slapping his gloved hands eagerly against his thighs. "They're mine, Monsieur," he said. "They're mine, and they're coming with me."

He motioned to his junior to lead the two prisoners out, then he struck a pose, as if he had just thought of something else. "Oh! By the way, M. Chaix," he said, "we might as well pick up your wife while we are at it, when she returns, eh? We might need her to corroborate your story, mightn't we?"

18.

By the end of the school year Oliver Benoit was able to breathe a sigh of relief. He had not been made to repeat the Fourth class, he had begun to make a few friends and he was on holiday for nine weeks. His parents were talking of a vacation to Spain or Greece for two weeks and he had the run of the garden at Le Bouton d'Or for the rest of the time. One of his friends from England had written too, asking if Oliver could come to stay for a week in July. The long summer holiday looked more promising than he had dared hope when first he had been brought to France.

And there were still the two children. He had seen them several times, usually at night in the courtyard or by the pond on the lower terrace. They were never far from his thoughts and he longed to see them again at close hand, to talk to them, to ask more about their lives, and why they had remained in the garden, but he feared he had frightened them off by being too inquisitive.

He had asked his father for a tent which he planned to sleep out in during the summer. He was sure he would be able to gain the confidence of the strange pair if, like them, he spent more of his time in the garden. He would clear a patch of ground near the pond, close to the bay tree where he had first seen them and pitch his tent there, where they would be bound to come to him.

On the first day of the holidays, however, a storm swept across the valley below the house and washed the garden with a fine, dense rain which made it impossible to do any of the things he had planned. He stood at his bedroom window wondering where his two strange friends were sheltering and if he could help them. He pictured the girl, in her flimsy dress as usual, and her brother in his shorts and socks and the sandals with all the holes in them. He turned away and wandered off, intending to watch a video, wishing he had asked a friend to come for the day and hoping the weather would improve.

And the weather did improve. "We're in France, Oliver," M. Benoit had told him on the second day of the storm. "It is July, we are in France and tomorrow the sun will shine. Tomorrow you will be pitching your tent in the garden, and maybe one of your friends from school will come to stay for a night or two."

As usual, his father was almost right. The sun shone brightly next day, but the ground was still too wet, even under the tent, and Oliver had to spend one more night in his own room.

He made up a camp bed, however, on a ground sheet on the floor of the tent, and at last, on the fourth day of his vacation he slept in the garden, alone and secretly a little nervous, but exhilarated with the feeling of independence that comes from sleeping on one's own in a tent for the first time. At last, he felt, the garden had become his private territory and he slept as if he had not rested for days, lulled by the flapping of the palm fronds and the babble of water trickling from the bronze trout in the arms of the boy-fountain.

The morning dawned fresh and crisp. Inside the little tent the air was warm from the heat of his body and the canvas above his head trembled gently as if moved by the sounds of the birds. Oliver stirred and turned over, opening his eyes to inspect his surroundings. Through the flaps at the end of the tent he could see the pond and beyond it the wall of the terrace where the leaves of the plane trees cast a green light across the garden. He sat upright suddenly. The flaps, he thought. The flaps are open. But he had tied them shut last night. Perhaps his father had been down already. How else would they be open?

He looked at his watch. It was not yet six. His father would hardly be out of bed.

He pulled his legs from the sleeping-bag and lowered his feet to the ground, then slipped his body over the edge of the stretcher and knelt beside it. He had crawled only halfway to the opening of the tent when he saw the flowers, an untidy handful of white daisies strewn on the groundsheet, almost as if they had been tossed in by someone in a hurry to get away. He picked them up slowly, gathering them together into a posy which he placed on his bed. He crawled a little further forward and poked his head out through the flaps. The terrace was deserted. A plump blackbird fled as his head emerged from the tent and the goldfish, which had been nosing the surface of the pond for food, dived for cover.

Oliver stood up outside the tent and looked around him. There was not a sign of life from the house. His parent's bedroom was shuttered and no lights shone in the kitchen. Not a sound could be heard, even from the street at the other side of the house. He shook his head and rubbed his eyes. He turned back to the tent, stooping to look inside at his bed and the unaccountable flowers still lying there. He picked them up and inspected them more closely. They were freshly picked. The moisture of their sap still oozed from the broken stalks and pinheads of dew clung to the velvet petals. They could not have been gathered more than a few minutes ago.

It had to be the children, he knew that. But this was different. This was a sign of friendship surely, more than simply allowing themselves to be seen in the garden or even appearing in his room. They must want to talk to me again, he thought, to become friends. He wished they had stayed for a while, so he could have asked them questions and told them about his own life. He didn't want friends who just gave him flowers while he slept and then slipped away.

Tomorrow, he told himself, I'll invite someone over, Tomas perhaps, or Philippe, and we'll take turns to keep watch, all night if necessary, until we see them. Then we can talk to them. Surely they want to talk to me as much as I want to talk to them? They must be so lonely here without their parents.

But even as the thoughts passed through his mind he knew he did not want to share the young pair with anyone. He knew no one would ever believe his story. It was too strange, too easy to ridicule. He recalled the last conversation he had had with the children and all the strange things they had told him.

"Not since our father went away," they had said, and, "The police came looking for us," and, "We never really left this house." None of it had made sense. He needed to know more. But now they had brought him flowers. They would come to him again, he knew. Then he would understand it all.

19.

Oliver did not speak to his parents of the flowers that day, nor indeed of the children. His father was still talking about the squatters and what a good thing it was they had gone, and Oliver was not certain enough about the children and everything they had told him to raise the subject with his parents, especially not with his father, who believed almost nothing and was suspicious of anything he did not understand.

On his second night in the garden Oliver did not close the flaps of the tent and he arranged his camp bed so as to be able to see out into the garden. The evening was warm and still and the garden was alive with the sounds of wings and the scratching of small feet. Through the leaves of the plane trees the sky was scattered with stars and a wedge of moon hung away to the east, half hidden by the cedars and pines which lined the slope of the hillside. Oliver could not have been more awake. He lay on his back listening to the buzz of the night, and when he heard the scuff of feet on the grass he sat up anxiously, but it was only his father coming to check that all was well and to say goodnight.

"Not frightened, are you?" M. Benoit asked. "Not afraid of anything?"

"No," Oliver replied. "There's nothing to be afraid of here."

His father reached out and put his hand on the boy's shoulder. "Happy on your own, are you?"

Oliver thought of nodding agreement. At least it would stop

the conversation, but then he sensed that his father's mood was easier somehow, and he decided to risk telling him about the children.

"I'm not on my own," he said, finally. "I've got friends here. The two children you think are squatters, but they're not." His voice was as casual as he could manage. "They're rather strange though, a boy and a girl. They live here, in the garden I think, but I don't really know enough about them. They left me some flowers last night so I suppose they like me." It all sounded rather silly explaining it like that, and he fell silent, relieved that it was too dark for his father to see him. M. Benoit bent down, fumbling at his torch. He switched it on and shone the light on to Oliver's face.

"They brought you flowers?" he said. "They live in the garden? Come on," he laughed. "Children don't live in gardens. And flowers. You must have been dreaming. Why would anyone bring you flowers?" Oliver made no reply. He knew only too well there was no explanation, and to tell his father everything he believed would only make it all sound even more ridiculous.

"Are you sure you're all right?" asked M. Benoit. "Wouldn't you rather sleep in the house tonight?" He seemed genuinely concerned.

"No," Oliver reassured his father. "I want to stay here. I want to see the children. I know there is something funny about them, but they did bring me flowers. They seem to live in the garden. They're not like us. They look like us, except for their clothes that is, but there's something different. I can't explain it. The girl told me they had lived here for a few days, I think she meant a long time ago, but now they seem to be here only part of the time and I don't know where they sleep or live. I've looked everywhere, all over the garden, but there's nowhere." He grimaced when he had finished his little speech, as though he could hardly believe it himself.

"Are you trying to tell me you think they're ghosts or something like that?" M. Benoit turned his torch on again, resting it upright in his hands to light the roof of the tent. "There are no ghosts, Oliver," he said. "Ghosts are invented by people with wild imaginations. You know we don't believe in any of that stuff."

"I don't know whether I do either." Oliver didn't want to sound too convinced about ghosts. "It's just that I don't understand what they're doing here or who they are. They aren't normal children, though. I do know that. Even their clothes are strange. Anyway, I think I'll be able to find out more if I sleep out here more often. I know they are here, or they were last night. Nobody else could have left the flowers. I'm going to try to stay awake all night in case they come again, and if I fall asleep I'll wake as early as I can in the morning. They want to talk to me, these children. I know they want to talk."

"I wouldn't be too sure about it, Oliver. Sometimes you know, when you're alone or a bit lonely, you imagine . . ."

"I'm not imagining anything, Papa! You would believe me if I told you what happened! What I saw last winter!"

"What? What happened last winter? Where?"

Oliver recounted the story as well as he could remember it, the unexpected appearance of the children in his bedroom, the words the pair had used and all the strange things they had told him, and then finally their sudden departure. It sounded even less real somehow, repeating it again after so long, and eventually, when he realized his father no longer believed him, he stopped talking and turned away. "Goodnight, Papa," he said. He settled down to wait.

He lay awake for several hours that night, finally drifting off to sleep in the early morning as the moon passed over the house, but even as he lay dormant the garden remained deserted, no timid figures approached through the grass, not a footfall could be heard on the steps nor even the faint snap of a daisy being plucked from the root of its mother-bush. He knew they would come eventually, that they wanted to talk. He was prepared to wait for them. And he knew too that he would have to wait alone, that the children would sense the disbelief in his father, and would not come if he was present.

And they did not come that night. It was not until Oliver was alone the next day that he saw the boy, standing, almost hiding it seemed, in the clump of bamboo beside the drive and looking out at him furtively as if to check if he was unaccompanied. The girl was there too, further back in a patch of shade, her hands clasped behind her back.

Oliver stopped. He smiled at the boy, holding out a hand towards him, beckoning him to come forward. But the boy did not move. He glanced behind Oliver's back, seeming to seek reassurance. Then he spoke, in his strange precise accent. "I would like to talk to you tonight," he said. His voice was a mere murmur. "We could meet here," he continued, "in the bamboo. Please come alone."

"There's no one with me," Oliver replied. "Only my father, for a while last night."

"Yes. We saw him. We did not think he would understand. It would be better if you came alone."

"What time will you be here?" Oliver asked.

"We are here all the time," replied the boy. "We will be here whenever you come." His sister nodded in agreement.

Oliver said nothing to his parents. He went to the tent and waited until the sounds from the kitchen had ended and his parents had gone upstairs. Then he got up and left the tent.

He made his way up the steps to the courtyard and along the drive. There was enough moonlight to see by. A warm breeze softened the air, the long fronds of the bamboo rustled softly and the scent of honeysuckle drifted past his face. The two children were there already, sitting in a small open patch of ground covered with dry leaves, the boy cross-legged and his sister beside him, her legs tucked away under the skirt of her white dress.

Oliver sat down with them, his heart racing so fast that he could not utter a word. The boy, Alain, spoke first. "We have been wanting to talk to you for a long time," he said. "Since we saw you that day when you came with your parents, in the days when the squatters were still here. Do you remember?"

Oliver replied with a nod. He could not speak. He did not trust his voice to hold firm.

"And then that night in winter during the storm," the boy continued, "we tried but you did not seem so friendly then. You kept asking questions and you didn't seem to believe anything we said to you, but you are still our only hope. We are relying on you. There has been nobody else here for years except for the squatters," he went on. "No one we could talk to."

"Why do you want to talk to someone?" Oliver asked. "Who are you? What are you doing here?"

"It is a long story," said the boy. "We didn't know anybody in Montélimar who might have helped us. We were afraid to talk to anyone."

The girl, Marie she had said her name was, spoke then. "Our father told us when he went away that we should not talk to anyone. And then he didn't come back. We stayed here all the time. At first we were so sure he would come back for us, but after a while, we gave up hope. We knew he was not going to come."

"What about your mother?" asked Oliver. "And what did you mean about the police, and that your names weren't really Alain and Marie? I don't understand any of it. I don't even understand why you want to talk to me. Who are you?" He knew he was beginning to sound angry again, it was all beyond him. The children made no reply.

"Tell me who you are," he demanded, almost shouting. "Tell me what you want. I will help you but I don't know where to start."

"Yes," said Alain. "We must tell you everything. I can see that." He settled himself on the ground and began to talk.

"Well, the first thing is our names aren't Alain and Marie. We are Jews. Our names are Jean-Pierre and Lucie Cohn and we come from Paris. I think we are orphans but I don't know for certain. Our mother is dead, we do know that, but our father left us here a long time ago. He isn't a brave man. He let my mother die, then he deserted us. I don't like him much. I don't like to think about him."

Beside him his sister shook her head in disagreement, but

the boy went on. It took most of the night for the details to unfold. Sometimes, in places, the children's voices stopped completely as the memories overcame them, and from time to time they sobbed, clutching each other as if they could not go on, but by dawn it was over and Oliver Benoit knew almost everything there was to know about M. Leon Cohn of Paris and his children and the death of his wife Madeleine.

20.

The heat in the crowded second class carriage of the train was unbearable. There were more than twice as many people as there were seats and most of the passengers had to stand. Guards stood at intervals along the aisle and at either end of the carriage, and many of their prisoners squatted or lay on the floor, or stood at angles against the walls in positions of discomfort. Outside the carriage the midday sun glared from a clear sky, but the windows were sealed with paper glued to the inside of the glass and the passengers could see nothing.

For the most part the people being deported from Vichy France were an unexceptional assortment, more men than women, and perhaps more young than old, but they could have been chosen from any street in any town in southern France. Their clothes were the drab clothes worn by everyone during the summer of 1942 and for the most part their shoes were well worn. On their faces also were many similarities. They were alert and restless and impatient, and fear lurked in the corners of their eyes.

Some, however, stood out. A few sported minor injuries, and one or two wore clothes which showed signs of a rough arrest. Leaning against the end of a row of seats, a swollen blue bruise across his cheek, was Leon Cohn and next to him Paul Chaix, with the fresh scab of a cut shining red on his temple.

The train contained prisoners headed for Paris, Jews mostly, together with a few members of the resistance groups who had been unlucky enough to be in the hands of the Vichy police at the time the message came through from Laval's office. It was almost as if Laval did not want the authorities in the northern sector to think he was weak.

In Paris, at dawn a couple of days earlier, the police had taken thousands of Jews from their homes and crowded them into the *Vélodrome d'Hiver*. Soon the holding centre at Drancy would be almost full too. The Nazis were doing well in the Occupied Zone and Vice-President Laval was determined to do equally well in his part of France.

Since 1941 his Commissariat of Jewish Affairs had kept records of the whereabouts of all the Jews in his zone, and when the opportunity came, he acted. The policy imposed by the Germans on the northern sector would apply, he decided, also to Vichy France. Everywhere Jews were arrested, whole families of them, and the trains to Paris were full. What the Nazis did with them after that was not Laval's problem. There were factories, huge factories in eastern Europe, which needed labour for the war and the Jews had no other work so it all made sense.

Somewhere north of Lyon Leon Cohn and the man who called himself Paul Chaix found space to sit on the hard floor of the railway carriage. The Jew from Paris and the man he had met in Montélimar had known each other for less than two days and Cohn thought wryly to himself that the only thing he knew for certain about his companion was that his name was not Paul Chaix. But they were men of almost the same age and their disastrous journey of the previous night had only served to strengthen their brief friendship. Not for one second had Chaix shown any sign of blaming Cohn for the accident in the boat, although they both knew it had been the fault of the man from Paris.

He was no sailor. As a child he had boated on the Seine with his father, but he would never have pretended to be familiar with the things which are second nature to those who grow up near water. It had been his fault, he knew, his inexperience which had led to the accident with the oar. And his companion on the train, the man who had risked his life to help him get away, was paying the price.

These thoughts stayed with Leon Cohn as the train rattled north to Paris, but they were not uppermost in his mind. There a hideous confusion reigned, in which the image of his wife's death fought for dominance with the knowledge that his children might still be locked in the tower at Le Bouton d'Or, and that by now their supplies of food and water would be exhausted. He hardly dared think about it, but Captain Desmarais had told them he was going to look for Chaix's wife, and if she had been caught too, what would happen to the children?

During the hours they had spent with the police in Le Teil, and later with the militia in Montélimar, the children had never been far from his mind. He had thought at one time of telling the captain about them, of asking him to send his men to release them, to set them free to face whatever might be decided for them, but he could not bring himself to tell Desmarais. He knew, or thought he knew, what was going to befall himself and Chaix, and Mme. Chaix as well if they had found her, and he could not condemn Jean-Pierre and Lucie to such a fate. Surely, he hoped, they would be able to get out of the hide-out, or someone would hear their cries. Perhaps the woman, the wife of Chaix, had returned earlier than planned. Perhaps she had avoided capture, had been warned by friends of her husband's arrest and had managed to get to the children and free them. The chances were good, he told himself, that they would be found, and by friends. It was a gamble to say nothing, but one he was prepared to take. He prayed that God would protect his children.

It had been only five days since Leon Cohn had left Paris with his family, but the knowledge of what had been happening since his departure had changed everything. He did not want to disown Paris or try to convince himself that he was no longer a Parisian. He wanted to believe that his friends and perhaps even his relatives were still there, in their apartments and houses, and on the streets. He even hoped to see familiar faces at the *Gare de Lyon*. He was not prepared for the scene which greeted him on the night of his return to the city.

A section of the station had been sealed off and surrounded by police guards. A drab convoy of canvas-covered trucks was drawn up beside the end platform and more guards stood about, some with dogs leashed to their belts or wrists, others with guns cradled warily to their chests as if they feared their unarmed prisoners might overwhelm them.

The passengers were bundled from the train and into the trucks without delay to set off rattling through the hot twilit streets in as much discomfort as if they were farm animals. From time to time Leon Cohn caught glimpses of the city through the canvas flaps of the truck's cover, but even in the warm half-light the familiar grey buildings and the summer-leafed trees seemed to cower from the soldiers and police who thronged the pavements. The city seemed to have lost its spirit. In only a few days his Paris had died.

The scene in the *Vélodrome d'Hiver* was a nightmare come to life. Thousands of anguished people were crammed into the building, holding grimly to the sad bundles of possessions they had been able to save from their houses or apartments, as if whatever treasures they contained would in some way act as anchors to the past against the heaving sea of humanity which now engulfed them. Loudspeakers crackled occasional messages to the assembly, drowned by the urgent hum of worried voices which filled the stadium and the insistent wailing of children, some still in arms, who cried from fear while their parents sat or stood about in attitudes of despair, most of them too distraught to offer comfort.

From time to time a section of the building would be cleared, its occupants pouring out through an exit door like sheep herded from a pen, to be replaced almost immediately by a new flock, distinguishable from its predecessors only by its nervous unfamiliarity with its new surroundings.

Into this maelstrom, late in the evening, Leon Cohn and Paul Chaix entered, exhausted by the long journey and a night without sleep, and immediately fearful in the atmosphere of hopelessness which filled the grim building. Cohn's eyes searched the sea of faces for a glimpse of someone he knew, colleagues or friends, perhaps even his mother-in-law, but there were so many people and the crowd was so dense he knew it would be almost impossible to find the old lady, even if she was there.

It was sometime during the night, with fear and hunger

churning his stomach, that he realized he would not be returning to Montélimar. He knew Mme. Chaix might not have got back to the children and that he must report their whereabouts to somebody. He himself had checked the strength of the door to the room in which they had been hidden, and the working of the padlock. There was little possibility of anyone finding their hideaway, and less of anyone breaking down the door. Equally there was no way for the children to let themselves out. They were trapped and except for himself and Paul and Mme. Chaix, no one knew they were there.

What was he to do? If he told the police of their presence Lucie and Jean-Pierre could be found, and like him, deported from Vichy France, but M. Cohn did not expect to be allowed to wait in the *Vélodrome* while his children followed him to Paris, and he dared not contemplate their fate if they arrived in the stadium alone. He had already seen the fearful faces of other children without parents. There was no alarm, no panic about them, merely a blankness, a cold acceptance of doom, a lonely fatalism which no stranger could soothe.

And if he did nothing? He closed his eyes against the thought. There was little enough food in the basket they had left for the children, and water for only a day. He had to act.

In the semi-darkness of his vast crowded prison he staggered to his feet, but a black curtain of unconsciousness descended over his eyes and he fell to his knees in a half faint. Still he did not sleep.

Later the sounds of the morning roused him from a torpor which was not sleep. He looked around, despairing of how to resolve his dilemma. Armed guards stood about in pairs or small groups and he knew he had to approach one of them. But at best they were unfriendly, some, the more senior officers, wore the distant brutal expression he had seen on the face of the captain of militia in Montélimar. He studied the faces of those nearest him. Few of them would meet his eye, and those who did appeared to take his gaze as a challenge.

He chose a man about his own age, one with children himself perhaps, who stood apart from his fellow guards. He picked his way over the sleeping bodies of his fellow prisoners. The man saw him approaching and turned his back. Leon Cohn had to work his way around him in order to face him.

"Good morning, Monsieur," he began. The guard turned away again, forcing Leon Cohn to step over an old man and woman who lay in each other's arms on the dirty floor.

"Good morning, Monsieur," he tried once more. "I need to talk to someone in authority. Can you help me, please?"

The man levelled his gaze at Leon Cohn, but he did not speak, allowing his eyes to travel down the prisoner's crumpled clothes, the shirt rumpled and stained from the water of the Rhône, and the trousers, not his own, which had somehow grown much too large for him, hanging loosely from his waist and gathering in baggy folds at his ankles.

Cohn tried again. "I need help, Monsieur," he said. "Or my children are going to die. They are hidden away. They have not enough food or water. Someone must get to them. They are in Montélimar. I would go to them myself but I don't expect that is possible."

The guard laughed once, a short scornful bark from which Leon Cohn could draw no sympathy. He felt a hand on his shoulder and turned in alarm, but it was Chaix, the cut on his temple swollen and dark and his clothes in disarray also.

"It's true," Chaix confirmed. "I hid them. The house is unoccupied and they will never get out unless someone helps them. They will die there. You must help us."

The guard stared at the man from Montélimar, blue-eyed and fair, then he turned to Leon Cohn, taking in his dark hair and sallow skin, the aquiline nose below the brown, frightened eyes. "You're a Jew." He spoke as if to confirm to himself something distasteful.

Leon Cohn nodded.

"And you expect us to let you go to Montélimar and get your children out of some hide-out you put them in. And then what? On your way to Spain, I suppose." He brought his face towards Leon Cohn's, so close their noses almost touched. "No, Monsieur," he whispered. "I don't know how you were picked up down south but you had your opportunity when you were in Montélimar. It's too late now to ask for favours. Anyway, the authorities in Vichy France aren't letting Jews back any more, so it's out of the question for you to go back even if we let you. And your children couldn't stay there either. They'll be sent up here as soon as they are picked up." He straightened his belt and looked away to indicate the end of the conversation.

Cohn raised his hands to grip the man's forearms. "No!" he said. "That's the problem. They won't be picked up. I don't expect to be allowed to go back myself, but surely someone could talk to the authorities in Montélimar, ask them to get my children out." He clasped his hands in a gesture of despair. "They will die, Monsieur, if someone doesn't get to them! They will die as surely as if I had starved them to death! Please, Monsieur." His voice was growing frantic, he began clutching at the policeman's sleeves again, willing him to listen.

The man tried to shake himself free of M. Cohn's hands. "For God's sake leave me alone!" he said, angered by the other's persistence, and stepping back.

But M. Cohn would not stop. "You must listen," he cried. "You must do something!"

Paul took Leon Cohn's hands in his and wrenched them from the arms of the guard. "He's telling the truth," he confirmed. "They will die if they are not released. They are in a house near the centre of the town. It's called Le Bouton d'Or. They are in a little tower in the garden. There is a door, padlocked, to the upper room. The Montélimar police know the house. It would take only a few minutes, and the children would survive."

"Please, Monsieur, you must telephone Montélimar," Leon Cohn interrupted. "They have already been there a whole day longer than we expected. It is most urgent."

The man shook his head as if to indicate that the problem was beyond his control, but M. Cohn would not let him go, crowding in on him, imploring him in sobs and whispers and cries to listen, to do something, until the man pushed back in anger, brushing M. Cohn's hands from his body. "All right!" he yelled. "Stop pawing me! Get your hands off me! I'll try to get a message to Montélimar, but it won't be easy. The telephones are busy enough without using them for calls about a couple of brats who have been locked up by their own father. Now, go away! I can't do anything until I'm off duty."

Paul Chaix took the arm of his friend, pulling him away, back to the piece of floor which had become theirs. "Sit down," he said. But Leon Cohn was too disturbed to sit. He stood, shivering, his arms wrapped around his body as if to ward off a chill. Chaix placed his hands on Cohn's shoulders. "That man will help," he said. "I'm sure of that. The children will be fine. They might even be up here soon. You might see them walk in through that door tomorrow morning."

"No," replied the other. "No. That would be too good, too much to expect. Just as long as they are freed. That's all I ask."

Three hours later the guard's shift was over. He left the great crowded hall. He stood outside on the pavement in the late morning sunshine and lit a cigarette which he inhaled carefully for a few minutes. Then he stretched his arms and fingers, and yawned and stood up high on his toes. Finally, he tossed away the smoking butt, climbed on to his bicycle and rode home to lunch with his wife and his children.

21.

Lucie and Jean-Pierre shared the remainder of the bread and the last apricot in silence. There had been no sound of life in the house or garden since the police had left. During the day the sun's rays had warmed the plaster dome above their room and the air inside had become hot and close. There was not a breath of wind and except for the scent of roses drifting in through the tiny window, they might as well have been enclosed in a bottle. Even the bees and birds seemed to have been stunned to drowsiness by the intensity of the heat. The only creature to disturb the stillness had been an inquisitive lizard which crawled panting into the shade of the window-ledge, eyeing them warily for a few minutes before subsiding into a restless sleep.

"I'm thirsty," Lucie complained. "I wish Papa would come back, or Mme. Chaix. I want to get out of here."

Jean-Pierre nodded. He was worried too. Two or three hours late he could understand, but it was after four o'clock. He had taken off his pullover and sandals and lay stretched out on the floor on an untidy pile of blankets. He was more worried than he cared to let his sister see. It was not so much the lateness of his father but the fact that the police had been to the house as well. What had happened to make them come searching, and on this day of all days? It puzzled and disturbed him.

And what might have happened to his father? He was a very organized man. He kept appointments carefully, he never made promises he could not keep, he forgot nothing, birth-days, anniversaries, all the milestones which marked the life of a family. It was simply not possible that he would not come back for them. He recalled the last words his father had spoken before he went away. "I will see you both in the morning," he had said, and in spite of his weaknesses his father had always been a man of his word.

Lucie began to cry again. Jean-Pierre sat up and held out a hand to her. "Please don't," he said. "He hasn't left us. He will be back soon, or the woman will come for us. Something has delayed them, that's all."

"You made him angry with us." Lucie turned her tear-stained face to her brother. "All those things you said to him yesterday, about Maman, how it should have been him instead of her who got shot. I was watching his face. You made him very unhappy. I think he has gone, I think he has left us here. What are we going to do? We can't stay here for ever. I'm hungry and there's no toilet. I want to go into the garden. I don't like it here. I don't want to sleep here again."

"We can't go anywhere by ourselves." Jean-Pierre was holding both her hands in his, shaking her, disagreeing with her. "We have almost no idea where we are. We have no money and no food. Where would we go? We have to stay here. What if he comes back and we are gone? He won't know where we are."

Lucie pulled her hands from his grasp and stood up, facing the inside of the locked door and clenching her fists until her little knuckles shone. Then she began to hammer wildly on the wooden planks, crying out in despair as flakes of old paint fell from the door almost as if it was shedding tears at her predicament. "Papa! Papa!" she cried. "Let us out! Don't leave us here! You must come back. Please come back, Papa! Jean-Pierre didn't mean it. He wants you to come back, too." She looked behind her at her brother. "Come on," she said. "Help me. We must try to open the door."

Jean-Pierre got to his feet and, standing beside her, put his weight on the door, pushing as hard as he could. But there was not a movement, not the slightest give of the door in its frame. It was shut fast, held by the heavy bolt outside, and the bolt was securely padlocked.

Suddenly aware of their predicament, Jean-Pierre too began hammering on the inside of the door and calling out, directing his voice to the window above them, but there was no reply, no sound at all came back to them. It was as if the unrelenting sun had withered all life in the garden, as if the entire world had deserted them and outside the little domed room, where yesterday there had been dappling trees and bright flowers and birds, there was nothing. Not a living soul. The silence dragged on, stunning the children into a drowsy, dejected emptiness. For hours they lay on the floor, their throats dry with thirst and their stomachs aching for food, until they fell into a light sleep. But they slept fitfully, dreaming of things a child's mind should not have to dream of, and waking often, and tossing the blankets on and off their bodies, uncertain even if they were warm or cold.

They tried again the following day to break down the door, but its strength, in which Paul and their father had placed so much confidence only two days earlier, had turned against them. They were imprisoned in the domed room. There was no way out.

They began to sleep for as much of the day as the night. There was nothing to occupy their minds but thoughts of their parents, and both children were trying to keep those thoughts at bay. Their mother was dead and their father had gone away. They wept with the desolation of orphans. From time to time they would lift their heads at the imagined sound of a footstep on the stone staircase outside, or the rustle of the wind as it disturbed the trees, but such moments of hope grew fewer as the hours passed and on one occasion, on the fourth day, when a dog came sniffing at the foot of the door, Jean-Pierre did not even bother to sit up. He knew his father had gone and would not be coming back, that the sounds he heard were just another dream, or another policeman, and he fell back to sleep. Beside him his sister slept too, her father's rose clutched tight in her hand as if she had used it on one last desperate wish. The water from which it had drawn life had gone, evaporated to nothingness in the heat, leaving only a powdery smear of salt to line the inside of the jug.

On the evening of the fifth day Lucie Cohn died. She lay curled peacefully on her side, a smile so entrancing fixed on her face that for a long time Jean-Pierre did not realize she had left him. One hand had fallen limply behind her head, a row of tiny marks on its palm where the thorns of the rose had penetrated her skin. The flower lay broken on the ground, its petals glowing like discarded jewels about the stem and its pollen clinging like gold dust to the child's pale fingers, but the thorns had not harmed her, the wounds were dry, there was no blood.

Jean-Pierre, too weak to sit, reached across and placed his fingers on hers. She was cold. Already her skin had the texture of paper. He gathered the petals of the rose from the floor and scattered them over her face. Then with the last of his strength he pulled the corner of a blanket over his head in order to block her from his view. In his own small cell of darkness he drifted off, first into a tranquil day-dream and later a long serene sleep. A few hours later he too was dead.

22.

The scene at the second railway station was even more alarming to Leon Cohn than that which had greeted him two days earlier on his arrival in Paris. Except for the ten or twelve truckloads of prisoners brought from the *Vélodrome d'Hiver* and a cordon of guards, the station was virtually deserted. It might have been out of use. Unoccupied trains stood idle at several of the platforms, no passengers sat on the waiting benches or walked about or met under the clocks, even the station staff seemed fewer and less busy than usual.

At the end platform, however, stood a drab line of carriages attached to an engine which, unlike the others at the station at that hour, was ready to move, its firemen and driver busying themselves around its grimy black carapace. The carriages were unmarked, their windows blacked out with dark paint and they were old.

Inside, unbeknownst to the intended passengers, the seats and partitions and racks had been removed, for there were to be no comforts on the way east.

To Leon and Paul it hardly seemed possible, as every new morning unfolded into yet a new horror, that each day could be worse than its predecessor. The journey had seemed interminable. For almost three days they had been crammed, more than two hundred of them, into a space which might once have held seventy people in moderate comfort.

There were more stops than they could bother to count. At rare and irregular intervals the doors of the carriage were dragged open and boxes of food and cans of water sufficient for less than half the number of travellers were shoved in. Those far from the doors sometimes got nothing, but for Leon Cohn, feverish and weak, the sight of daylight was better than any food, and Paul Chaix managed to keep him supplied with enough water to keep him from unconsciousness.

The train stopped often and for long periods. There was no explanation of their whereabouts or destination. The only discernible change was that at each stop as they travelled further east, the guards, German soldiers and the occasional black-uniformed S.S. officer (for they were no longer in France), had become more brutal, jabbing the barrels of their rifles in through the open doors of the carriages to amuse themselves it seemed, causing chaos inside the train as those behind struggled for a glimpse of air and those at the doors tried to retreat.

The long journey ended almost in anti-climax. Early on the morning of the third day the train stopped for three or four hours, but no one could sleep. Unfamiliar noises could be heard in the distance, the sounds of other trains stopping and starting, the clanging of coupling hooks and the grinding and squealing of wheels on track as brakes were applied. Finally, when it seemed as if they might wait for ever on their siding, they moved off, before coming to a stop again in less than five minutes. The doors remained closed, however, for another half hour, while they listened to the sounds of dogs snarling and the crunch of footsteps on gravel, the dragging of many weary feet and orders being barked at unseen people, in German mostly but in other languages too, unfamiliar to Leon Cohn and Paul Chaix.

It was mid-morning by the time the doors were flung open and the flood of light into the carriage came as a shock to the travelling prisoners, but there was little time to catch their breath. Outside the carriage stood a line of soldiers, several holding dogs which struggled on the ends of their leads, gasping in their efforts to get at the prisoners. Others, those who had flung back the doors, were armed, with bayonets fixed to their rifles. They bellowed insults at the dazed passengers as if they wanted to heighten their fear, ordering them to jump from the carriages and bludgeoning those who hesitated with their rifle butts or in some cases prodding them with the steel of their bayonets. It was, Leon Cohn thought, as if the wild beasts of some imagined hell had been unleashed in human form on to the fearful occupants of the train.

They stumbled down as best they could, young girls and old men, women protective of children in their arms and young men, weaponless and disoriented, shamed by their impotence. They formed a listless group on the windswept concrete platform, the occupants of the separate carriages joining up in a disordered cavalcade, marshalled into shape by the guards before being marched off in the direction of a forbidding gateway set in a tall fence of barbed wire. It was not until they passed a gap between two carriages that Paul Chaix caught a glimpse on the other side of the train of the ornate, well-maintained building which served as the railway station.

There was a sign on the platform in a language which a few of the passengers recognized as Polish and below it a translation in German. AUSCHWITZ, it read.

A hubbub of questions arose from the prisoners. "What language is that? Where are we?" And, "Auschwitz? Where is

Auschwitz? Are we in Poland?'' The guards herded them along, a slow shuffling procession of random humanity, surrounded by dogs and guns and whips and truncheons, breathing with every step the stench of pollution, of furnaces, of factories and refuse, breathing with the fear of those for whom the smell of death is close at hand.

Beneath a murky sky they could see smoke churning from the tall chimneys of distant factories and to one side, nearer them, rows of long, low wooden huts which looked like dormitories. They came to a halt at the rear of a queue of prisoners. Cohn could hear yet another group falling in behind them, the whole broad line moving forward continuously in the direction of a crude office above which flew the sinister flag of the S.S. Outside the building stood a pair of German officers, elegantly uniformed.

It took almost two hours before they got to the front of the queue but it was clear long before then what was taking place. The old men and women were being turned off to the left, along with those who were unable to stand or walk without assistance. The able-bodied, children and adults alike, went to the right. To what it was not clear, but it seemed to Leon Cohn unlikely to be death, not so soon anyway.

Despite Paul Chaix's injury they were not sent to the left. They were marched away towards the complex of buildings which looked like dormitories, dazed by the ease and speed with which the choice between life and death had been made.

Those prisoners fortunate enough to have been turned to the right were herded into a rough concrete building and ordered to strip. Their clothes were carried away in huge bundles by other prisoners wearing grey and white-striped uniforms of coarse cloth. Their watches or jewellery or other possessions were taken from them. Their heads were shaved and their teeth were inspected. They were made to stand in long lines under a crude system of showers from which gushed foul-smelling water bearing chemicals which burned their wounds. Then they stood in lines, naked and shivering, as their own uniforms were handed out to them in sizes which seldom bore comparison with the height or girth of the wearers. Finally, towards the end of the afternoon, when they had completed the process of dressing, they were led off again to their huts, to the sullen welcome of other prisoners trusted to keep them in order. Throughout the process, Leon and Paul managed to remain together as if they had been friends since childhood.

The leader of their hut was a Jew from Warsaw, a stockily-built man in his early forties, who stood on a step to address the new arrivals. "My name is Ziff," he announced, in good French. "I am not a friend of the Germans but I run this hut the way they want it run. That way I might survive, and so might you. Any other way and the chances are we will all finish up in Birkenau, so you do things the way I tell you."

Leon Cohn raised his hand like a schoolboy new to a class. "Please?" he called. "May I ask a question?"

"Not yet." Ziff did not even look at him. "You will be working at the Farben factory, starting tomorrow morning. They make fuels there. We leave at six. If you are late you are off the work team. That probably means you are finished here." He waved his hand towards the row of small windows which lined one side of the hut. "Birkenau is in that direction," he said. "That's as far as you can go here. Let's hope none of us ever sees it. You get up on time, you are ready on time, you work as hard as you need to, you don't fight and you don't argue with the guards. And finally," he raised his voice to a shout. "You don't try to escape!"

He stopped to look at the men facing him as if to reinforce his words. "You," he said, looking for M. Cohn's face among the crowd. "What did you want?"

"I want to know if it is possible to communicate with our families or anyone outside the camp?"

There were snorts of derision from all sides and laughter, but Leon Cohn was not going to be stopped from asking his question. "I left my two children behind, in Montélimar. They are going to die unless I can get a message to the police. Is there any chance I can make contact with the police in France, to tell them where my children are hiding?"

Ziff looked at M. Cohn, smiling in amazement. "What's your name, friend?" he asked.

"Cohn. Leon Cohn. I'm from Paris but we were caught in Montélimar. My wife was killed and my children are still there, locked away, but they will starve unless someone gets to them." He looked around him expectantly as if he anticipated a wave of sympathy from the other prisoners. There was hardly a sound.

Ziff shook his head slowly. "Monsieur Leon Cohn from Paris," he said, "do you know where you are? You are in Auschwitz, in Poland. You can't hope to make contact with France. I'm sorry about your children, but don't waste my time with questions like that." He turned away, signalling the end of his speech, then as if thinking better of it, turned back again to face his audience. "Would everyone here who would like to find his family raise his hand?" he asked.

Leon Cohn looked around, almost eagerly at first, as if he thought he might receive support for his request, then in embarrassment, as he saw the forest of hands rising around him. There was hardly a man in the room who did not have his arm lifted to the ceiling.

"Forget about France, Monsieur. As far as France is concerned you don't exist any longer." Ziff clapped his hands together loudly, signalling the end of his speech. "Go to bed, all of you," he said. He nodded at M. Cohn, not unkindly. "Does anyone know him?"

Paul put a hand on his friend's shoulder and returned Ziff's nod. "I do," he said. "He's with me."

23.

Dawn was almost breaking as Oliver Benoit crawled into the tent, but he had no intention of sleeping. As soon as he heard the sound of a kettle being lifted and a tap running he got up from his bed and ran to the kitchen.

"Can we talk?" he demanded of his father. "You've got to believe me now!" Something in the boy's determination made his father listen and Oliver had already decided to tell him everything. "I was talking to my friends. The two children I told you about. They were in the garden. We sat in the bamboo. I know everything about them now. I'd like you to help me with them. They need help. They want me to find out what happened to their father. He disappeared during the war and never came back. They are dead, the children I mean. They are ghosts." To his surprise he found he could say the strange words as easily as if he were saying, "they're English," or, "they're fat." He sat on the edge of the kitchen table, almost too excited to care if his father believed him or not.

"They are ghosts," he repeated. "Do you want to hear all about them?"

M. Benoit stood stock still, a cup of coffee at his lips, his mouth open with surprise. "No, Oliver," he said. "You must stop this now. I'm not listening to this nonsense. Do you really expect me to believe that there are ghosts in our garden, and you have had a conversation with them? No. I don't want to hear any more of this."

"I have just been with them," Oliver protested. "In the

bamboo. We spoke for hours. Why should I make it up? It is true. Everything I'm telling you is true. But it won't ever be true for you because you won't believe it *could* be true. That's why they won't ever show themselves to you. You have to believe it. I'm not sure I can do what they want on my own. I need your help."

M. Benoit shook his head, not to show he would not help, but from disbelief. He had never before seen his son so convinced of anything. "Tell me more about what you saw. Tell me everything. What are their names? Where do they come from?"

"They came from Paris during the war, but they died here, in Le Bouton d'Or, in the tower in fact. Their names are Jean-Pierre and Lucie, their surname is Cohn. They were Jews. Their mother was shot . . ."

"Jews!" M. Benoit exclaimed. "They were Jews?" He lowered himself slowly into a chair, puzzled now, rather than angry. "What on earth are you talking about, boy? This isn't funny, you know."

"They are really nice," Oliver insisted. "The girl is very nice and Jean-Pierre is, too. It's just that he doesn't like his father much. He thinks his father left them to die. That's why he wants to find him. They both do. M. Cohn could still be alive. He was thirty-eight when he left them, he'd only be eighty-six now."

"No," said M. Benoit. "I don't like the sound of this, Oliver. I don't like it at all. I don't want to hear any more of ghosts and Jews and children dying. Here in this garden. It's all nonsense. You're making it all up or imagining it. You've got to stop it. I don't want to hear another word about it." He put both his hands behind his head and tautened the muscles of his arms. "Now, what are you going to do today? Is there anywhere we can swim, or a tennis court?"

But Oliver did not want to change the subject. He could think of nothing but the children and their story. "I don't want to go swimming or play tennis. I told Jean-Pierre I would see what I could find out about his father, about this house during the war too, who owned it and all that stuff."

"Well, I'm not going to allow you to waste your holidays looking for a ghost's father," M. Benoit said. "It's not going to be much fun here for your mother and me is it, if that's all you're going to do." He jumped to his feet. "I'm going to get something to eat," he announced. He pulled open the door of the refrigerator and began searching the shelves diligently.

"Well, I'm not going swimming today!" Oliver half-shouted at his father's back. "I'm going to spend the day in Montélimar!" And M. Benoit, sensing the purpose in his son's voice, did not reply. He got out some eggs and a frying pan and studied the boy's face intently. Without another word he began cooking and soon the smell of melting butter brought Mme. Benoit down from her room, yawning and dishevelled in her dressing-gown.

She looked at her bleary-eyed son. Oliver sat with his elbows on the table, his head resting in his hands. "You didn't sleep, either?" she asked, smiling at him. "You look terrible. Did they keep you awake as well?"

"Did what keep me awake?" Oliver asked. He turned to face her. "What do you mean?"

"Those kids," his mother replied, "in the garden. God knows where they came from. They didn't seem to be doing any harm but I could hear them all night, chattering away. I couldn't get to sleep. They must be those squatters' children back again. I thought we'd got rid of them, but they were there all right, at least two of them, maybe more. You'll have to search the garden today, François, to make sure they've gone. We don't want them setting up home again here."

Out of the corner of his eye Oliver could see that his father had turned to stare at him. He knew he should say nothing, ask no questions, and presently his mother spoke again. "Didn't you hear them, François? They went on for hours, nearly drove me mad."

"No," said M. Benoit, keeping his eyes on Oliver. "I didn't hear a thing. And I was awake for a lot of the night. In the garden, did you say? Whereabouts in the garden?"

"I couldn't tell exactly. I got up to look out of the bedroom window and I could hear the voices quite clearly, children's voices. They seemed to be coming from somewhere along the drive, near that patch of bamboo, I think."

This time Oliver stared at his father. M. Benoit was looking puzzled now, unable to meet his son's gaze, concentrating on his fried eggs as if all of a sudden they had acquired an unexpected importance.

Mme. Benoit spooned coffee grounds into a jug. "If they're there again tonight we'll have to call the police," she said. She poured a stream of boiling water from the kettle on to the coffee, "or the next thing we'll have the whole lot of them back, parents and all. If they're not here already, that is."

Nobody spoke for a while after the threat to call the police. M. Benoit seemed stunned by the news that his wife had heard the children's voices, and from the direction of the bamboo, too. And now Oliver was worried, more concerned to keep the police away than with convincing his father of what had happened.

"Who owned this house before we bought it?" he asked, looking at his parents as if he had forgotten about the voices in the garden. "Why don't we find out about them and the squatters and why the house had been empty for so long. I'm interested in this house."

"I can't remember the full story," M. Benoit said. He spoke cautiously now. "The *notaire* told me some of the history, but I've forgotten most of it. There was a family called Peyron who owned it before us, but they hadn't lived here for years, not since the war. I didn't meet old M. Peyron, Georges was his name, when we signed the contract to buy the house, but his wife told me he grew up here, and after the war he was going to move back, but it was too big for them so it was left empty for almost fifty years, until we bought it. She said he used to come back at first to feed the goldfish and pick flowers, but he stopped after a few years. Apparently he didn't want to live here again."

"Do you know where he lives now?" Oliver pressed his father for more.

M. Benoit shook his head. "I can't remember exactly," he said. "Some small village, out towards Grignan, I think. He's very old. Why do you want to know? He can't have had anything to do with those children."

"I'm just interested," Oliver replied. "I might do a sort of project on the house," he added, getting quite carried away. At least his father no longer disbelieved his story so completely. "You know, who built it, who lived here, who died here, that sort of thing."

M. Benoit sat silent as his son continued. "Especially now we know the house was empty for so long, except for the squatters and their children. What was the *notaire*'s name, Papa? He could help us, couldn't he? To find M. Peyron, I mean."

"Yes. I suppose he would know where to find him." M. Benoit was not prepared to argue any more. "I'll telephone him if you like."

But when M. Benoit telephoned he was told the *notaire* was on vacation until the end of August and no one else knew anything about old M. Peyron who had owned the house called Le Bouton d'Or. After the call they sat, father and son, eyeing one another uneasily, but when his mother left the room Oliver spoke quietly and directly to his father. "You do believe me now though, don't you, about the children? Maman would hardly have made it up, would she, especially about them being in the bamboo."

M. Benoit said nothing. He stood up and led Oliver out of the house, deep in thought. He inspected the ground around the tent, and the trees and flowers. He climbed the steps leading to the drive and walked to the patch of bamboo from which his wife had said the voices came. There was no sign of life, no clue to the whereabouts of the children, nothing. "All right," he said at last. "It might be true, but there's no proof they are ghosts. They could easily be ordinary kids like you, just pretending to be ghosts. I'll have to see them myself. I won't believe anything till I've actually seen them myself, and heard their voices and spoken to them."

24.

The department of France in which Montélimar is situated is called le Drôme. It is a thinly populated area of farms, small villages and few large towns. It did not seem likely to Oliver Benoit that a search for a M. Peyron could be an impossible task, but telephone directories in France are laid out so that each village or town has its own section, and Oliver soon discovered that it could take many days to find the M. Peyron he was seeking. There were Peyrons everywhere, in all the cities. In Montélimar and Valence, in Crest and Romans-sur-Isère and in many other of the smaller villages and towns. Unless you knew where a man lived it could take for ever to find him in the directory.

He got out a map and looked for the line of villages which straddled the road from Montélimar to Grignan. M. Benoit shouted again that he was pretty sure the *notaire* had said towards Grignan, so Oliver began the search there, looking for the names of all the villages. He drew up a list of ten at first, thinking that if he drew a blank with those he would cast his net further afield with the next list.

He had no success that first day and it was not until almost mid-morning the following day that he made a contact. A woman's voice answered after a long delay, an old cracked voice, which shouted at Oliver that she was deaf and he would have to talk more loudly. She confirmed that her husband was M. Georges Peyron, and yes, he was the same M. Peyron who used to live at a house called Le Bouton d'Or in Montélimar.

"Could I please speak to him?" Oliver asked.

"What about?" she demanded to know.

"I live in the house now. I wanted to ask him some questions about it. It's for a project I'm working on," he lied again. "I think he's the only person who could help me."

"He doesn't want to know about that house," the old woman said. "He is very old now. I don't want him disturbed with a lot of questions about it. He left there when the war began. He needed a vegetable garden during the war and there was no vegetable garden there, only some fruit trees. When we were married, after the war, we decided not to move back to Montélimar."

"But it's the war time I wanted to ask him about," Oliver persisted. "I'm sure he could help me. I need to know who lived in the house during the war. I think somebody was living there. Did he rent the house to anyone?"

"Never! The house was empty. After the war my husband went there from time to time to keep an eye on it, but no one lived there." She paused. "I know all about it although I wasn't married to him then. It wasn't a happy house for him," she went on. "Many strange things happened during the war you know, sad things. It's not good to remind him of those things now. I hope you will be happy in that house. You are living there with your family, are you? What did you say your name was?"

"Benoit," said Oliver. "Oliver Benoit. Are you quite sure there was no one there during the war?"

"Absolutely," the old woman replied. "There's nothing to know about Le Bouton d'Or during that time. We never talk about it. Goodbye." Oliver frowned as he heard her replace the receiver.

"Well, what did she say?" his father asked.

"She said the house was empty during the war, but I'm not sure I believe her. She didn't want me talking to her husband either, she said he was too old. She said it had not been a happy house for him. I believe that part of her story but I'm still sure her husband could help us. I want to go and see him. Where are they? Valaurie des Colombes, isn't it? That's not far. I could go on the bus this afternoon."

25.

The road from Montélimar traverses the mouth of a valley which opens out to the east of the city, widening and rising to meet a range of mountains which protects the valley from the worst of the winter mistral. The land is rich in tall trees and luxuriant grasses, and in summer two rivers and countless streams meander through its lush fields and woods.

Beyond the hills to the south, however, a different country begins. The trees are stunted and low. Rocky outcrops and stony fields mark the landscape, and in a dry summer the small streams which feed the crops can vanish for weeks beneath the floor of the valley. It is the beginning of the harsh landscape of Provence.

It would make little sense, Oliver thought, for a man accustomed to the fertile warmth of Montélimar to move away, to settle in the more barren land to the south, unless he was driven away, or there was something he wished to leave behind him, something he wished to forget. But M. Georges Peyron had left. He had not returned to live at Le Bouton d'Or after the war. Something must have happened, Oliver thought, to make M. Peyron leave such a beautiful house for ever.

After the bus had driven off the boy stood looking northwards. Valaurie des Colombes lay above him on a hill beside the road to Grignan, a small settlement of about thirty ancient houses with a couple of shops and a bakery, built on a jumble of narrow winding streets. The bus had dropped Oliver at the side of the main road and he had had to walk a few hundred metres up the dusty road which approached the village. By the time he had reached the crossroads which marked the heart of the small town he was hot and tired.

Only one shop was open, attended by a girl Oliver recognized from school. She looked up from her magazine and greeted him without enthusiasm. "I'm looking for a M. Peyron," Oliver said. "He lives somewhere around here."

The girl stared at him blankly for a time before answering. At last she spoke. "Why?" she asked.

"I want to talk to him. M. Georges Peyron. I think he can help me with some information."

She looked at him in surprise. "You want to talk to M. Georges Peyron."

"Yes. Can you tell me where he lives? I know his house is somewhere in Valaurie, I telephoned his wife this morning. I've come out on the bus to see him. From Montélimar."

"You've come to see old M. Peyron," said the girl, "to talk to him." She seemed to be almost laughing at Oliver. He was beginning to find her annoying. His request was hardly extraordinary.

"Yes," he said. "I have. Which is his house?"

"He lives across the road." The girl smirked. "The house with dark blue shutters. I'll show you." She put down her magazine and walked to the door of the shop. She pointed to a stone village house with a door opening on to the street less than twenty metres from where they stood. "That's it," she said. "Good luck. If he talks to you it will be the first time he has spoken to anyone for ages. He never speaks. My father has lived in this village for twenty years and he's never heard him say a word."

"Thank you anyway," Oliver said. "I might as well try now I have come this far." He walked across the road and knocked on the pitted wooden door. It was opened by an elderly woman in a flowered dress. She had the gnarled hands of someone whose life has been spent at work. A mass of silver hair was dragged into a tight bun on her neck. She did not look unfriendly, but she was tall and forbidding. She did not smile. Oliver was struck silent at the sight of her, the words he had planned to say sticking in his throat.

The woman spoke before he did. "I suppose you are Oliver Benoit?" She spoke the words as a question. "I half knew you were going to come. I'll have to tell you now, why I put you off, I mean. I'm afraid your journey has been a waste of time, but come in anyway, it's too hot to stand outside."

She motioned him into a dark-walled room. The louvred shutters were closed tight against the hot afternoon sun and there was no other light. A long brown sofa stood to one side of an immense stone fireplace and opposite it were two chairs upholstered in brown corduroy. Above the fireplace hung an oil painting of a basin with a fountain playing in its centre. The surface of the basin was covered in water lilies and the fountain was a bronze statue of a small boy holding a fish to his breast.

"Our pond," Oliver murmured. He walked to the picture to examine it more closely. "It's still exactly like that," he said, turning back to the old woman. "We've even got the fountain playing again. Who painted it?"

"My husband used to be a good painter," the woman said.

"Only an amateur of course. When he lived there he painted pictures of every part of the house and garden. Then when he came here at the beginning of the war he brought only two paintings with him. This house was too small to take them all. All the others were lost or stolen during the war."

"Where is the other one you kept?" Oliver asked.

"Oh," she looked hesitant, "we haven't got it here any more. We threw it out in fact, soon after the war. My husband decided he didn't like it. He found it quite upsetting, having it in the room."

"What was it of?" Oliver thought he already knew the answer, but he wanted to be sure.

"Really, I don't like to talk about it, not in front of him," the woman said, turning away.

Oliver looked around, startled, in the direction of her gaze. In a corner even darker than the rest of the room a figure sat huddled in a heavy-legged chair, swathed in blankets as if it was the middle of winter. "My husband," said the woman. "M. Georges Peyron."

The figure in the chair might as well have been made of wax as flesh and bone. The blankets did not rise and fall with his breathing, not a whisker of his moustache moved with the expulsion of air from his nose, nor even could the faintest murmur of breath be heard from his partly-opened mouth. The old man was as still as a corpse.

Oliver stared in awe. "Oh," he said, "I'm sorry. I didn't realize he was there."

"It's all right," the woman said. "You weren't to know." She beckoned Oliver into an adjoining room. "I told him you telephoned this morning. I told him what you wanted. He usually refuses to have anybody in the house while he is up, but this morning when I told him about you, after you telephoned, I got the impression he wanted to see you. I was going to try and find you myself, but here you are.

"I'm not saying you'll get any information from him either. He doesn't talk at all any more, just nods or shakes his head sometimes. You won't be able to get him to speak, but with some people he likes to listen and I think he wants to listen to you."

She put a hand on Oliver's arm. "Be gentle with him, please. He's very frail and he gets upset easily. Go on." She pushed the boy back towards the dark room.

Oliver almost crept back into the room where the old man sat. He found a stool and pulled it towards the heavy-legged chair. He sat down and looked at M. Peyron's face. There was not a sign of life, no indication that the old man was aware of the presence of another person in the room. It was difficult to know how to start. He sat silent for some time, collecting his thoughts before speaking.

"My name is Oliver Benoit," he began. "My parents have bought a house in Montélimar. We moved there in January. The house is called Le Bouton d'Or." There was no movement from the old man, but Oliver continued. "I think you know the house. There is a picture of the pond above your fireplace. The pond is still there, M. Peyron. You should come to see it one day. It is still very beautiful, just as you painted it."

The old man remained as still as a statue. "Your wife said you had painted a lot of pictures of the house. There was another one here, she said, but you told her to throw it away. I know why you didn't want to keep it, M. Peyron. I think it was a picture of something you didn't like to remember."

Oliver was beginning to lose hope of getting any response, but he tried once more. "It was a picture of the tower, wasn't it, the little tower in the garden with the dome on its top?" He stopped and studied the old man intently. There was not so much as a flicker across the worn face, not a spark in the tired eyes, but Oliver sensed a change. Perhaps it was no more than the slightest increase in the rhythm of M. Peyron's pulse, but he felt certain the man could hear his words.

"There were squatters in the house when my parents bought it," he continued, "and there were children. I thought at first the children belonged to the squatters but now I know they had nothing to do with them." This time he saw the old man move. One hand, which had appeared to be lying easily on the arm of the chair, had tightened, the skin showing taut across the knuckles as the old fingers gripped the wood.

"I want to help those children, M. Peyron. I need to know who was living in the house during the war. Whoever was there would have known the children and what happened to their father. His name was Leon Cohn and he disappeared in 1942, in July. I must find out what happened to him. I promised his children I would do that. But I can't do it without your help. I must find out who else was in the house."

M. Peyron nodded very slowly, but he said nothing. He could have been agreeing with Oliver or simply asking him to continue.

"Did you ever know a man called Paul?" Oliver asked. "I don't know his surname. Perhaps he used the house sometimes during the war?"

The old man's head snapped upright, thudding on to the back of the chair. Oliver saw his hands tighten again. There was no doubt the name Paul meant something to him. "Tell me about Paul?" he demanded. "What is the rest of his name and where can I find him? Is he still alive? He is very important. He was the last person to be seen with M. Cohn. If I could talk to him I think I could find out what happened."

The old man's mouth began to move awkwardly, as if he was trying to chew the air, but no sound came from his lips.

"Please M. Peyron. Please help me!" Oliver's voice was raised. The woman came into the room wiping her hands on a cloth.

"Oh," she said. "What have you done? You've got him into a terrible state. What have you been asking him?" She took Oliver's arm and pulled him from the darkened room. "You won't get any more from him today," she said crossly. "You'll have to go."

"I'm very sorry Mme. Peyron. I didn't want to upset him. I think he could understand what I was saying, though. I think he wants to help me. I asked him if he knew a man called Paul, a long time ago, in 1942."

"Paul? Paul who?" she said. Oliver returned her steady gaze. "So," she went on, "you know about Paul, do you? How do you know about him at your age? How old are you, twelve or thirteen? How on earth could you have heard of Paul?"

"It's something I heard from the children at Le Bouton d'Or. They told me there was a man who went away with their father, who was with him on the last day they saw him. They said the man's name was Paul."

"When did this happen? There's been no one living in that house for years, since long before you were born. Since the start of the war."

"It was during the war, Madame, in 1942. I know it's all true. The children told me all about it."

"What children? There are no children in that house except you."

"There are, Madame, in a way. Two of them. In the garden. I've talked to them. They died there during the war. It was terrible."

Mme. Peyron bent down to look at him. "These are things we haven't spoken of for years, young M. Benoit, things we do not want to remember. You must not joke about them. Terrible things happened during the war, you know, to most of us in France, even those who simply lived a quiet life as best they could. For some, for those such as my husband, it was unimaginable. Many people were captured and shot, or taken away to the concentration camps. Many more were tortured beyond what they could stand.

"Others, those who were not with my husband, live in shame still, for what they did not do. His first wife was captured by the militia and sent away to the Nazis. He never saw her again. Many of his friends too were caught and many innocent people died, some of them children. It is not something to make jokes about, children, dead children, in gardens. Stop it, do you hear! If that is what you have come here for I will not help you." She stopped talking. She stared hard at Oliver as if she was trying to read his mind and shook her head. "But you are a strange fellow. What is it you want?" Oliver was silent.

"I think you want something different, young M. Benoit," she continued, nodding to herself and staring fiercely into the boy's face.

"All right," she said at last. "I will talk to my husband for you. I will talk to him because he needs help. The doctors can do nothing for him. Every year he grows worse and every day I pray for him. He prays too. Every day he prays to die, but he cannot die. He continues to live, with his memories. God knows what sort of a life it is for him."

"But Paul, Mme. Peyron? Where will I find Paul?" Oliver found himself crying with despair, in front of a woman he hardly knew. He wiped his sleeve across his face.

"You have already met Paul," said the old woman. "That is Paul, or what is left of him." She pointed to the figure hunched in the chair in the room next door. "That is M. Paul Chaix."

26.

Oliver lay on the grass of the terrace. The sun beat through the canopy of leaves above his head, dappling his body with a soft light. He lay completely motionless, still too confused to move. It had been two days since his visit to the house of M. Peyron. The old woman had told him he could come back, but not for three or four days. "He gets too tired," she had said as he had left after the first visit. "He'll need a long rest after this."

Oliver had told his parents everything that had happened. Even his father was beginning to believe his story. "I know it's impossible," M. Benoit had said as they sat together one morning, "but I do think there's something going on. I do believe they are here. Your mother didn't make up the story about hearing them in the garden, but I don't understand it. I don't know what's happening any more. I would still like to see them myself."

"I think they might be afraid of you," Oliver told him. "They said something to me when I saw them earlier this week about not coming to the tent if you were there."

M. Benoit shrugged. He looked disappointed, but Oliver made no further comment and his father turned away.

"Perhaps they are afraid of you," said Oliver, "because they think you wouldn't really like them, that you would feel the same way about them as other people would, because they're Jews.

"Tell me what happened here, Papa, in France I mean,

during the war. If I am to help the children I need to know what happened. Did your parents ever talk about it?"

"No," M. Benoit replied. "No one ever talked about it, not for years afterwards."

He took off his glasses and laid them on the table. He rubbed his eyes slowly before continuing. "We had to keep on pretending, Oliver, that it hadn't happened, or that we didn't know it had happened. Some of us are still pretending. But everyone knew, all along, and not enough of them spoke out about it. It could have been stopped, you see. It could have been stopped.

"Both my parents were in Paris, but they were young then, only teenagers. It was a tough time for them, for everyone. The Germans occupied the city for five years and there wasn't much freedom, not much of anything, in fact. Food was scarce, especially towards the end and there was no petrol either, so getting around wasn't easy. It was almost impossible to leave the city."

"And the Jews. What happened to the Jews?"

"They all disappeared. By the end of the war there were no Jews left in Paris, or anywhere else in France for that matter. Hundreds of thousands of them had gone, many died. Some escaped and a few went into hiding, but most of them were taken away. Hardly any survived. It was a bad time."

"What had they done? Why were they taken away?"

"They were Jews, Oliver. That's all, just Jews." At first M. Benoit did not seem to realize that his son was waiting, that he needed to explain more. He went on. "People thought they were too rich," he said, "too powerful. There weren't many of them but they always seemed to get to the top, were always successful." He stopped talking, aware that his attempt at an explanation was inadequate, futile.

"I don't know why, Oliver," he went on. "There was no reason. The Germans, Hitler anyway, wanted to get rid of them and enough people in France felt the same way, so they co-operated with the Nazis. If anyone tried to oppose them, tried to help the Jews, they were treated as enemies, as if they were Jewish themselves. I had an aunt, the sister of my mother, who lived here, near Montélimar. I remember her telling me stories about Jews being rounded up and sent away, and others coming south from Paris in the early years of the war, how almost no one would help them. It was such a risk, you see. If you were caught helping Jews you would be deported or shot and your family would be badly treated too. Food was rationed then, and if you didn't qualify for rations, life became almost impossible. Only the bravest people risked their lives against the Nazis or the Vichy Government, and as for helping Jews ... well ... there were not so many brave people. It's impossible to know... If I'd been alive in those days..."

Oliver stared up at his father, hoping he would answer the unasked question which hung, almost visible between them. But M. Benoit was silent for a long time.

"What would you have done, Papa, if you had been alive then, in Paris ... or Montélimar?" The boy's hands were twisted together awkwardly as he waited.

"I don't know," said his father, eventually. "I wish I could tell you what I would have done, that I would have helped, but I can't say. I don't know. I am ashamed to say that I don't know."

27.

A fresh wind got up as the day wore on. By evening it was shaking the leaves of the plane trees and raising small eddies of dust from the corners of the courtyard. From nowhere appeared a layer of twigs and the dry petals of flowers which had bloomed earlier in the summer, settling around the bases of the trees and lying up untidily against the balustraded walls of the garden.

After dinner Oliver walked alone along the drive. A mongrel dog had strayed up from one of the houses in the town and it gambolled about him wildly, and sniffed at his legs and feet as if they had known each other for ever.

He hardly dared look at the clump of bamboo as he passed, nor into the long stone-walled tunnel which led to the spring under the hillside. He left the main driveway and pushed his way through the undergrowth which almost blocked the small paths criss-crossing the garden.

He could not acknowledge even to himself that he was hoping to see a sign of the two children and tell them what he knew; that he had found the man called Paul, the man who had seen the children so long ago, when they had been alive. He so wanted to tell them that, but he did not see them and when finally he turned to make his way back to the house he could not hide his disappointment.

Mme. Benoit tried to persuade him to sleep in the house that night. The wind was showing no sign of dying down and from the windows of the house she could see the tent rippling and swaying and straining at its ropes like a sailboat anxious to get under way. But her son wanted to spend another night outside the house, on the terrace.

For most of the evening the wind played about the tent, raising tiny ripples on the surface of the pond and stirring the bushes and flowers in the garden, making it impossible to sleep. The creatures which usually inhabited the terrace were nowhere to be seen, sheltering in their flimsy nests or below ground in the warmth of their holes. Only the mongrel dog, which had resisted all Oliver's efforts to drive it away, witnessed the setting of the moon and the flooding of starlight into the dark air.

After midnight the wind died away leaving in its place a silence so serene, so absolute, so utterly still, it was as if the world itself had fallen under the spell of sleep.

Disappointed at his failure to make contact with the children, Oliver slept too, as the stillness grew around him and the silence enveloped him like a blanket. The dog lay drowsing at the entrance to the tent, one eye open to the sky and snuffling from time to time with pleasure at having found itself a friend for the night.

Early in the morning, when the stars began to fade at the approach of dawn, the dog moved, pawing the ground restlessly in its sleep, and whining softly. No movement or sound caused the animal to wake, not the rustle of a leaf or the snap of a twig, not even the slow bursting of a flower bud or the tentative ruffling of a dove's waking wing. An onlooker outside the tent might have assumed that the dog was dreaming, that it would soon lie still again, but the onlooker might not have seen the cause of the dog's stirring, or sensed the movement at the entrance to the tent, or seen the handful of tiny roses, damp with dew and fragile scent, which appeared on the pillow beside the sleeping head of Oliver Benoit.

28.

The old man seemed to Oliver to be no more awake than he had been on his last visit. The room was as dark as ever, the blanket over his body as still as before and the ancient wiry hands rested on the arms of the chair so easily they might have been the hands of a dead man.

"It's good that he has had a few days rest," Mme. Peyron said to Oliver, "and he is better in the mornings, too. I have told him you know who he is, what he used to call himself during the war. I think he will talk to you if he can. I prayed all night that he will talk. It hasn't been easy, you know. He wasn't as bad as this when I married him. I thought he would get better with time, but he has got worse and worse. There is so much inside him, things he saw, things he can never forget. He has become like a frightened child." She touched the old man's forehead, letting her hand rest on him for a while before leaving the room.

She had placed the stool in readiness beside her husband's chair. Oliver sat down. He felt less nervous now. It was better to be alone, just the old man and him.

"Your wife told me you called yourself Paul during the war," he began. "Paul Chaix. I am looking for a man called Paul who spent some time at the house called Le Bouton d'Or, in 1942. I told you this a few days ago. Do you remember?"

The old man moved his head, it was not a nod, less than a nod, but it was a movement. Oliver continued. "A man was

brought to the house with his two children, a man called Leon
Cohn. The children were called Jean-Pierre and Lucie. They
met a man in that house who was called Paul. I think, M.
Peyron, that you are the Paul I am looking for." The man's
head moved again, but this time it seemed to shake from side
to side as if he was denying everything.

"It has taken me a long time to find out all these things M.
Peyron, but I know almost everything now. There is only one
more thing I need to know and you might be able to help me. I
want to know what happened to M. Cohn. Please say you
know, that it was you who went with him when he left his
children."

The old man bit his lips hard, sucking them into his mouth
as if afraid they might speak if he let them loose. He shook his
head once more. He said nothing.

"I have seen the children, Monsieur! I know it sounds
strange but they are still there, at Le Bouton d'Or. I have seen
them often. I have even talked to them. You believe me, don't
you? How else would I have known about you, about Paul? I
know how they died, too. They told me about being hidden
away in the tower. But they are blaming their father, especially
Jean-Pierre. He thinks his father was a coward, that he
deserted them, left them to die. I can't believe that, M.
Peyron. You have got to tell me what happened to M. Cohn.
Perhaps he is still alive? Perhaps you know where he is?"

This time the old man shook his head vigorously for a long
time, then, exhausted, he let it fall back to rest on the cushion
behind him. "No," he said at last, in a voice so quiet Oliver
could hardly hear it. "Leon Cohn was not a coward."

"Is he alive, Monsieur? Can you tell me where he is?"

The worn old face of M. Peyron trembled as if an agonizing pain had struck him. "No," he said. "He is dead."

"How did he die, Monsieur? If he was not a coward I would like to tell his children how he died."

"He was not a coward!" The old man's voice grew suddenly stronger, echoing so loudly through the quiet room that Mme. Peyron rushed from the kitchen.

"What is it?" she asked. "Who is talking?" She took in the scene, her husband's eyes filled with angry tears and the boy, leaning forward almost eagerly, urging the old man on. "What is happening?" she cried. "Is he talking?" Her hands clutched at her cheeks, then her chest, as if to control her breath. "Oh, my dearest God!" She stood motionless, staring at the scene in disbelief, unable to speak. When at last she found her voice again she could only murmur so softly that for a while Oliver could not make out her words. "He is talking. He is talking. Thank you. Thank you. Thank you," she whispered, again and again, but Oliver had no idea who she was speaking to. He did not take his eyes from the old man's face and when the woman stopped her murmuring her husband began again.

"I want to see these children," the man said. "I must talk to them."

"They are at the house," Oliver told him. "They are there all the time. I see them often. I will show you where they are."

Mme. Peyron put a hand to her mouth, a worried expression on her face. "No, Georges. It's not possible for you to go to Montélimar." She turned to Oliver for support. "He hasn't been away from Valaurie for years, he would never be able to make the journey. It would kill him. How would he get there?

We don't have a car, and the bus... It's out of the question."
She shook her head to let them both know how impossible it
all was.

But the old man was unmoved. He spoke slowly and
clearly, without taking his eyes from his wife. "I am going
back to the house," he said. "I am going back to Le Bouton
d'Or. I will tell the children of M. Leon Cohn about their
father." He put his hand on Oliver's wrist. "I will come this
afternoon."

"My father will come to get you," Oliver said. "If I explain
it all to him he will bring you."

29.

The long July day had been too hot for comfort, but by evening a breeze began to drift in from the east bringing with it the scents of the mountains where sheep run with their lambs among the herb-grasses and wild flowers. At the wind's cool touch the leaves of the plane trees, which had drooped in the blistering heat of the day, seemed to come to life again, lifting their faces to greet the breeze and waving a welcome to the freshening air.

In the pond at Le Bouton d'Or the goldfish swam with a new energy, leaping from the water as if they thought they were salmon, before plopping back and plunging to the depths at the base of the fountain to devour their insect prey at their leisure.

M. Benoit was full of apprehension as he watched his son seat the old man. The boy had placed a cushion on the flight of steps leading from the terrace up to the garden and when his guest had settled himself on it he spread a rug across the man's knees. M. Peyron sat with a walking stick between his legs, the handle protruding above the rug, his gnarled hands gripping it with the fierce intensity of anticipation.

"Are you comfortable, Monsieur?" Oliver asked.

"Yes, yes, yes," the old man snapped at him. "Where are the children of Leon Cohn? Tell them I'm here."

"I'm going now, to get them," Oliver said, "but I might be a while. I don't always know where they are. I have to find them."

M. Peyron nodded once, impatiently.

Oliver disappeared between the thickets of brambles and ivy which lined the path leading from the top of the steps. A bough which had been torn away from one of the cedars during the winter storms lay across the track, the palm trees had disguised it with their dead fronds and in the near darkness he stumbled into it, cutting his shin on its jagged end. He stopped to look up at the drive which ran parallel above him, hidden from his view by the clump of bamboo. He would look there first. He climbed the remains of the narrow tiers of stone set into the hillside, and made his way back towards the house to search the bamboo. But there was no one there.

He took another path away from the house and turned up a track which had once led to the upper terrace. There was a clear dry space under a chestnut tree where he had seen the children one evening many weeks ago, but it too was empty. He turned back, intending to cross the drive and search the lower slopes of the garden, when he caught sight of the girl's dress behind a shield of laurels, not more than a couple of metres from him. Jean-Pierre was with her, harder to see in his dark clothes and holding her hand. They stared at him as if he was a stranger. He could sense their fear, something was troubling them.

Lucie spoke before he could open his mouth. "Who is the man with you?" she asked. "The man your father brought here."

"What have you said about us?" Jean-Pierre demanded. "You said your father would not believe our story if you told him. And who is that old man?"

"He is the man you have been waiting for," said Oliver. "I

have found him. He is Paul, Paul Chaix. He knows about your father. He wants to talk to you. If you come with me, he is waiting by the pond. He can tell you all about your father."

"How do we know it is the same Paul?" Jean-Pierre asked. He was angry, upset. He pulled his hand from Lucie's and stood defiantly with his hands on his hips. "He'll have to prove he is the same man," he said.

Oliver saw no point in arguing. He set off ahead of the pair, winding his way down the rock steps and along the briar-tangled path, looking behind him every now and then to make sure they were still following, but when he arrived back at the seat on which he had left the old man the children were nowhere to be seen. He sat down on one of the low pillars which stood at either side of the bottom step. M. Peyron looked across at him, waiting for him to speak.

"They are coming, Monsieur," Oliver said. "They are a little frightened but if we wait they will come." He lifted his face to the cool breeze and closed his eyes. When he opened them, Jean-Pierre and Lucie were standing at the foot of the steps and M. Peyron had begun to speak. His voice was like the dry crackling of a newspaper which has lain a long time in sunlight.

"The dress," the old man was saying. "I remember the white dress with the red flowers." His voice was trembling as he pointed to Lucie.

He looked at Jean-Pierre, standing with his hands in his pockets and his feet apart, a scowl on his face as if he didn't care what the old man might say about him. "And the boy, who looks so like his father, why is he angry?"

"I'm not angry!" Jean-Pierre retorted. "How do we know

who you are to tell us about our father? You could be anyone."

"But I remember you, Jean-Pierre. I remember many
things about you. You are wearing the same clothes as you did
when I first saw you. And you were angry then, too. Nothing
has changed."

"Tell me something else then, something only you would
know. Not just about the clothes we are wearing now, or that I
look like my father. What did you leave for us, up there in the
tower?"

"My wife packed a small basket. There was bread, it was
probably stale, and fruit, apricots I think, and some water.
And there was a candle in the room as well. I remember the
candle."

"What else?" Jean-Pierre demanded to know.

"I don't recall anything else, nothing I left for you, anyway.
There was just the basket and some blankets."

"There!" Jean-Pierre curled his lip in triumph. "You don't
remember everything. There was something else left for us
and you don't remember it. I don't believe you are Paul."

M. Peyron spoke to Lucie, holding out a hand to her. "Is
that true?" he asked. "Was there something else?"

"Yes," said the girl. "There was something, but it wasn't
left by you, it was from our father." She stopped, appearing to
hope the old man would remember. He lowered his head,
studying the ground for a time before lifting his face to the
children.

"A rose," he said at last. "A rose the colour of a sunset. Of
course I remember."

Lucie fell to her knees. "I believe you are Paul," she said. "I don't remember your face but I believe you are Paul."

"What about your wife?" Jean-Pierre demanded. "Why didn't she come back, and our father too? He deserted us, didn't he? He left us here, locked away in the tower, to fend for ourselves. He let us die, just like he let our mother die."

"That's not true!" The old man leant forward, his face taut with anger, stretching out his feeble hand with the walking stick in it and waving it about as if he would like to strike the boy.

"I will tell you about your father," he said at last. "I will tell you things about your father no one has ever heard before."

30.

Oliver slipped off the pillar to sit with Lucie on the lowest step. Jean-Pierre stood a couple of paces back, still angry and hesitant, then, half convinced by the old man's memory of the rose, he knelt on the dry ground beside his sister. M. Peyron closed his eyes for so long Oliver thought he must have fallen asleep. When eventually he opened his eyes again and began to speak, it was with a question.

"What time of day was it," he asked, "when your father and I left? Was it late in the evening? I think I remember that, but now, after so long I'm not sure of anything any more. I still have a picture of the colours in my mind. Yes, it was evening, a beautiful evening too, but there was no moon. We walked out of town as if we were going on a picnic. We walked to Ancone. There were ducks on the riverbank and three mulberry trees. I had to show your father where the boat was hidden and how to get across the river to Le Teil. That's where it all went wrong."

The three children listened in silence as the story was told, of the accident in the boat, the capture of the two men by the police, of being handed over to the militia, of the train journey to Paris and the agony of waiting inside the *Vélodrome d'Hiver*. The old man spoke of their father's despair for them alone in the tower, of how he had risked the anger of the guard, pleading with him to get a message to the authorities in Montélimar. Then the story became darker, even more fearsome, as he spoke of the second train, worse than the first, and finally of their arrival in the camp at Auschwitz.

"You cannot imagine what it was like there," said M. Peyron. "Auschwitz was a city of slaves. Jewish slaves mostly, but from everywhere, from all over Europe, from Germany, from Poland, from Hungary, from Russia. Bulgarian slaves, Romanian slaves, Czechoslovakian slaves, Dutch slaves. Men and women, old and young, child slaves. Yes, boys and girls as young as you, younger even, some of them. I can never forget it. And of course French slaves too. Your father and I. We weren't the only French there, but we stuck together. We knew no one else." He coughed harshly into the palm of his hand. "Every day I thank God your father was there," he said. "For me the first few days were the worst. I thought I would go insane. But he who had lost everything he loved in the world kept me from going mad. I will never know where the strength of his spirit came from.

"I will not tell you all the things that happened in Auschwitz," the old man whispered. "What happened was too awful to remember, too awful for the ears of children. If you want you can read about it. There are books, plenty of books. It's better for me not to talk about it. I will talk only about M. Leon Cohn, because I must, because I am forced to." M. Peyron almost glared at Jean-Pierre, then looked up at the night sky as if he was not speaking to the children seated on the ground before him but to some other audience, unseen and distant, more understanding perhaps, an audience which knew already of Auschwitz and the terror which lodged in the hearts of men like Georges Peyron.

"He is dead," said the old man when he resumed talking. "Leon Cohn is dead. I will tell you of the last day of his life. That is all you need to hear."

31.

"There was a boy in our hut in Auschwitz. I suppose he was about your age." He looked at Oliver and then at Jean-Pierre. "He was Polish, from Warsaw. A Jew, Jean-Pierre, like you. He spoke some French so we could talk with him. His grandmother, I think he said, came from Strasbourg. He was in our hut in Auschwitz. Quite alone. He said his mother was there too, but in some other area. They thought nothing about splitting up families, so he had not seen her since the day he arrived in the camp.

"Leon Cohn befriended him, made sure he got his share of food, kept the bullies away from him. He used to show him a photograph of you, taken when you were much younger, in the happy days long before the war. You were sitting together on a single kitchen chair. He often talked about you to the boy from Warsaw. Perhaps he thought he was like you, Jean-Pierre, that if he helped this unknown boy someone might do the same for you. Anyway, the boy found a place to sleep near your father. It was good for each of them to have the other, you understand, and he was a nice boy, clever too.

"We had been in the camp for about a month when it happened. We used to have to walk to the factories each morning. It was quite a long walk, more than half an hour, and of course we got very little food so we were not strong.

"We had been assigned to the Farben factory which made synthetic fuels. The system was that all of us, the prisoners I mean, were owned by the S.S., and we were rented out to work in the different factories. That is what I meant when I said we were slaves. The S.S. was paid for our labour and as for us, we got nothing. The skimpiest of meals as long as we could still work, but those who were too ill or old, even those who had injured themselves and could not work for a day or two were sent to Birkenau. Birkenau was the death camp, where they killed the prisoners who caused trouble or could no longer work. It was not far. Sometimes the injured would even be made to walk there to die.

"Well, gangs of us would be walking to the factories every morning, long lines of slaves, trudging to and fro, some going, others returning. They worked twenty-four hours a day most of the time, those factories; it was very efficient, Auschwitz. We were always under guard, of course. The officers were Germans, from the S.S., and the rest, a mixture, mostly from eastern Europe, collaborators and thugs, villains all of them, the worst sort of people.

"The morning I am going to tell you about started like any other. We would have had a few scraps of old bread and some sort of a drink – it was not water but it just as well might have been water for all the flavour it had – before setting off towards the chimneys of the factory. There would have been about two hundred of us, I suppose, hurried along by the guards and their dogs, and all around us the other groups of prisoners, heads bowed, shuffling along. We all looked so weary, always weary, and there was never enough food, never a day when we were not hungry.

"On this particular morning another group was passing us, going in the opposite direction. We didn't usually bother with the other sections of the camp, there were so many people in

Auschwitz, it was huge, and it was better to stay with your own group, where you knew everyone. It became almost like a family. Sometimes one of us might recognize a person from another group who we knew or had seen before, but the guards didn't like us to talk to the other groups. All we could do was wave and hope they recognized us.

"But this time, Stefan, that was the name of the boy from Warsaw, thought he saw his mother. He stopped walking and shouted to a woman in the other group. It was pathetic. At first the woman couldn't hear him, but he kept on calling to her as she approached and the closer she drew the more he shouted until at one point, when she was less than fifty metres from us, the boy stopped walking. He would not move. One of the guards, a brute from the Ukraine, stopped behind him, prodding him with the barrel of his rifle, telling him to go on. The rest of us walked slower and slower. We had watched such scenes before. We were anxious for the boy.

"Leon Cohn and I were at the rear of the group so we were still quite close when the trouble started. The woman he had been calling was looking back at him. To this day I still don't know if she was his mother, but she stopped. Maybe she had a son of her own, maybe Stefan was her son. She waved to him. Her group stopped also and there we stood, two lines of prisoners watching as the boy and the woman called to each other and waved.

"At first, when they saw what was happening, the guards let the two go on for a while, but then the boy could stand it no longer. He began to move towards the woman. She had stepped forward from her group, holding out her arms to him as he ran. The Ukrainian put his rifle to his shoulder. Your father and I were directly behind him, just a few metres away. We thought he was aiming at the boy. Leon stepped forward, but we were too far away and the guard had plenty of time. He shot the woman first. Stefan must have seen her fall, but he kept on running. The Ukrainian took aim at him. Leon Cohn was quicker than me. He got to the guard and leapt at him, dragging the gun away and tossing it to the ground. The guard stumbled and fell, cursing. Leon and I were standing together as he turned his head to see who had attacked him. He got to his feet and brushed the dust from his uniform. The other guards were coming towards us, but the Ukrainian motioned them to stay away. He walked to his rifle and picked it up.

"He held it by the barrel and began walking towards me, his eyes never leaving my face. It was clear he thought it had been me who had attacked him. He raised the wooden stock of the gun high above his head. He was going to club me with it when Leon Cohn spoke.

" 'It was me,' he said, 'not this man.' He put his arm in front of my face to shield me from the blow. The guard hesitated. I was sure he was going to kill us both, but he hesitated. Perhaps it was because there were so many on-lookers and all the other guards were around us by then too.

"He lowered the gun, reversing it to its proper position, the stock in his hands and the barrel pointing at Leon. He was so close I could smell him. No one breathed. I was terrified. We had seen the Ukrainian kill prisoners before. He was completely without mercy. But he lowered the gun still further until it was pointing down towards the ground. He began to smile. I started to hope. Perhaps, I thought, he is in a good mood today. Perhaps he will do nothing.

"Then he fired. The bullet passed clean through Leon's foot. For a time he remained standing. The pain must have been unbearable, but he stood for as long as he could. Then he fell, crouching in a heap on the ground. I remember hearing him crying, and gripping his foot with both hands as if he could relieve the pain by touching it.

"The guard raised the gun at me as a warning. He did not take his eyes off mine. When he was sure I would do nothing he slung his rifle across his shoulders and waited. After a while your father looked up. I could see he was in terrible pain, but he knew he had to stand, and walk. He knew what would happen if he could not work. He caught hold of my knee to help raise himself. I put my hand down to him but the guard knocked it away. It took for ever, but Leon managed to get up again. He could bear no weight on his wounded foot but for several seconds he stood. God knows how he did it.

"Then he fell once more. The Ukrainian watched as he collapsed and he began to smile. He kicked your father. Three or four times he kicked him until he looked up. When their eyes met the guard was smiling broadly. He said only one word, very quietly, very softly, but there was such menace in his voice. All of us who heard him knew what he meant."

M. Peyron paused, unable to speak for a while. Then he lifted his face to the children and continued.

" 'Birkenau,' the guard said. Just the one word. 'Birkenau'.

"I was allowed to carry your father back in my arms. There was nothing to ease his pain, but I found some rags and bandaged his foot as best I could. He was unconscious for much of the day, but in the evening he came round and we talked.

"He spoke for hours about your mother, her name was Madeleine, wasn't it?" As he uttered the name Madeleine, M. Peyron seemed to wake as if from a trance, as if for the first time since he had begun his story he remembered he had an audience. "He talked of you, too." The old man nodded in the direction of Lucie and Jean-Pierre, although in the poor light it was difficult to see their faces.

"He made me promise I would come back to Montélimar to find out what had happened to you, and to look after you. I promised, although in those days we didn't know whether we would live for another minute or another day, let alone another year, or until the war was over.

"But I survived Auschwitz, and the war. I came back to Le Bouton d'Or. It was not until then I learned my first wife had been captured. The militia had known who I was as soon as they saw me in Le Teil with your father and they set a trap for my wife, waiting for her to return to this house. They caught her and tortured her, but she told them nothing, not even about you children. She did not know that I had been captured, of course, how could she have known? She thought Leon and I would return to let you out of your hiding place. That is why no one came back for you. There was no one else who knew you were here." He fell silent and lowered his head to the ground as if deep in thought.

"She was handed over to the Gestapo," he said, finally. "She was executed two years before I got back. You met her, do you remember?"

"Yes," Jean-Pierre murmured. "She gave us food. I remember her."

"That was the first thing I heard when I returned to

Montélimar, in 1945. And then I came back to this house. I was afraid to come because I knew what I had to do. Two days I waited before I opened the door to the little room in the tower. I had hoped to find it open, open and empty, but it was still padlocked shut. The door had not been touched since your father and I left you. I had lost the key, of course. I had to break down the door. Please don't ask me to tell you any more. Until the last minute I hoped for a miracle, that I would not find you, that the little room would be empty, but you were both there. The thing I remember was the rose. Everything else in the room had faded away to nothing except the rose. I saw it as soon as I opened the door. The petals were perfectly preserved. As vivid still as if they had just been picked. I gathered them up. I still have them."

In the dim light of a moon beginning to rise above the hills the three children could make out the movements of the old man as he reached into his jacket. He pulled something from the pocket, a packet or an envelope, and drew from it a piece of roughly-folded paper. "I wrote this in Auschwitz," he said. "It is a letter from Leon Cohn. He was too weak to write it himself. He spoke the words to me. It was the only paper we had and the pencil was very small but the words came from your father. It was our last night together. He was taken to Birkenau the following day.

"You read it, boy. I can't see in this light." He passed the paper to Oliver and sat back, pulling the rug close around his waist and allowing his chin to fall on to his hands as if his efforts had exhausted him.

Oliver opened the single piece of coarse brown paper. It was thick and the edges were uneven, the sort of paper a butcher might have used for wrapping meat. He turned it to face the light of the moon. The words were crammed together and the pencil handwriting was so pale as to be almost invisible, but as his eyes adjusted to the light it grew clearer and he began to read.

"My dear Lucie and Jean-Pierre,

"M. Paul Chaix, who went with me from Montélimar to help us escape, is still with me. It is the twenty-sixth of August, 1942, and we are in a place called Auschwitz. At the moment I am not well and Paul is writing this letter for me. I hope one day he will be able to explain to you why I could not write it myself, but life here is not easy and I pray each night that I will not have to stay much longer. I worry that when I left you there were some things between us which I could not explain, but these are matters it is best to leave until another day, and I have no doubt we will meet again one day soon, for, as your dearest mother used to say, we are remarkable people, we Cohns.

"But with things as they are it may be some time before I see you. I can only ask you to be patient. You will discover that time will make all your problems seem unimportant. All the things you are so certain of one day will be untrue the next. All of us judge people wrongly some of the time and later wish we hadn't, so let your judgements wait.

"But I am not writing to talk only of our mistakes. I am writing to tell you both that I loved you from the second you were born and that I never stopped loving you. I know, Jean-Pierre, that at the end, in Montélimar, you were angry with me. I pray that by the time you read this letter your anger will have passed and that your memories of me will be as loving as mine are of you.

"Goodbye, my dearest Jean-Pierre and my darling Lucie. I will never forget you."

At the foot of the letter Oliver could make out the name "Papa", but it was some time before he was able to read the word aloud.

M. Peyron reached out again, the envelope still in his hand. Oliver began folding the letter, thinking he wanted it back. Instead the old man shook the envelope at him almost angrily. "Take it," he said. "Take it."

Oliver took it from him. It was half open, the flap partly curled inside it.

"Open it," M. Peyron ordered him.

Oliver slid his fingers into the envelope, touching something cool and soft. He turned it upside down, the palm of one hand open beneath it to catch the unseen contents.

Jean-Pierre and Lucie watched him intently as a shower of rose petals tumbled out, bright as the sun, fluttering through his fingers to the ground to settle like glistening snowflakes upon the hard, stone steps. It was as if the trees of Le Bouton d'Or had dreamed briefly of autumn and turned to gold, to shed not leaves but burnished tears for the children of Leon Cohn.

It seemed an age before anyone spoke, and then it was the old man whose voice Oliver heard.

"Thank you," he said. He had one arm stretched out to the boy, the other gripping the handle of his stick as he tried to stand. "Thank you," he repeated. For a time Oliver did not realize it was to him the old man was speaking. He took M.

Peyron's hand to help him, taking his weight as he pulled him upright.

"I'm tired," the man whispered. "I never thought I would talk again for so long. You'd better take me inside."

"Can't you stay, Monsieur?" said Jean-Pierre. He knelt beside his sister among the scattered rose petals. "Please tell us more," he begged. Oliver had never seen the boy smile before, never seen contentment on his face.

The old man shook his head. "No," he said. "Not tonight. I must go."

"Another time, perhaps?"

"Yes. Perhaps I will come again," said M. Peyron.

Jean-Pierre nodded.

Lucie squeezed her brother's hand. "Now we can go, too," she said.

"No! No! Don't say you are going!" Oliver cried. "Please stay. I have no friends here except you."

"We have to go." Jean-Pierre looked at him calmly. "I need to think about my father now. Someone like you will have friends wherever you are, but we must go. Thank you for what you have done. You have freed us."

Lucie let fall her brother's hand and stepped forward, raising her face to Oliver's cheek. He scarcely knew whether she touched him. Her skin was light, as if a feather or a moth's wing had brushed him. "Do you think we might come back sometimes, to your garden?" she asked.

"Yes! Yes! Of course you can come back! You can stay here! Both of you! For as long as you want!"

She spoke again, as though from a distance this time.

"Goodbye, Oliver," her voice said. "I wish my mother had met you. She would have said you were a remarkable person."

Oliver lifted his hand to wave a farewell but the figure of Jean-Pierre Cohn was fading and indistinct. He turned back to the girl, reaching out to place a restraining hand on her shoulder, but she too could hardly be seen and his fingers touched nothing, slid freely through the air.

He felt the hand of M. Peyron on his arm. "Take me inside, please," the old man was saying. "It is all done now."

Oliver could not bring himself to leave. In vain he looked around for Jean-Pierre and Lucie, but they had vanished, disappearing as completely as if they had never been there.

Against the evening sky a dense flock of small birds rose as one, and swelled and fell as easily as a sigh. A gentle breath of wind disturbed the air, flitting across the terrace after the children, lifting the fallen petals of the fiery rose and dashing them, suddenly pale and dry and weightless, against the steps where they crumbled to dust and slid away down the cracks and holes of the stone stairway like the receding waters of a summer flood.

Then all was still in the garden. It seemed to Oliver that the earth was waiting, as if something was passing for which silence was the only welcome, as if to speak or even draw breath might disturb the peace drifting in from the south, where the moon hung pale above the hills, and the air was warm, and the buds of new roses unfurled their velvet beauty to the dark sky.